GUARDING
ANGEL

An unforgettable story of healing and forgiveness

A NOVEL

Darlene A. Williams

Guarding Angel by Darlene A. Williams

Additional copies may be purchased at **www.Amazon.com.**

Cover by Mae@ www.coverfreshdesigns.com .

PRINTED IN THE UNITED STATES OF AMERICA

DEDICATION

To my mother and grandmother. Thank you for always being there for me through everything, including the beginning of the writing of this book. I only wish you could have been here for the end. I am blessed that you were a loving mother and grandmother; I love and miss you both.

ACKNOWLEDGMENTS

I thank God for giving me the wisdom and courage to try my hand at writing.

I want to thank my daughter Alyssa for being patient with me during the writing of this book.

I want to thank my friend Carol for all the help and advice you have given me. I thought I had lost the desire to write long ago, at the passing of my grandmother in 1998 and my mother in 2001. You are the one who stirred up within me the desire to put pen to paper and finish this book. And for that I thank you.

You have truly been an inspiration and a Godsend; you are my guardian angel who came into my life at a time when I needed a friend the most. Thank you for the encouraging words. You are truly a special lady and great friend.

CONTENTS

PROLOGUE

It was a beautiful Sunday morning. I sat in the second row of the old country church that I loved from the moment I first laid eyes on it. A cool summer breeze blew through the open windows, giving the sanctuary an even more peaceful, calming effect. To my left sat my grandmother. She wore a blue dress which hung just below the knees, nothing special really, but it made her beautiful blue eyes sparkle. They reminded me of the dark blue of an ocean. I smiled when she placed her hand on mine and gave it a gentle pat, and then turned my attention back to the sermon. My heart filled with pride as Pastor Moore delivered his message with such deep heartfelt love and conviction that it sent chills down my spine.

I remember a time, thirteen years ago, to be exact, when the pastor was much different from the man he is today. He was once full of anger and grief over the loss of his wife and five-year-old daughter, due to the carelessness of a drunk driver. He had lost all faith in God and himself. So much so, that he was walking away from the ministry and closing the church for good. But you know what they say. God works in mysterious ways, and he used the faith and love of an abused child who was going through something so evil and horrific that it would soon change the life of not only the pastor, but also all who were involved.

That child was me, and this is my story.

CHAPTER 1

WAKING TO A NIGHTMARE

I awoke early in the morning, long before the sun came up, and lay staring out the window through a small opening in the curtains. The moonlight found its way in through the opening. Everything was quiet except for the occasional pop and creak of the house settling, and the sound of a mouse trying to gnaw its way through the wall. If he managed to get in, I hoped he went to Mama's room and bit her on the butt. I giggled as I snuggled further under the blankets. I pulled them over my shoulders and fell back to sleep. I was having the most beautiful dream, which was soon forgotten when I awoke to the sound of Mama's voice.

"Get up you little brat!" she screeched. She had a way of doing things. It was never in a loving manner, but always yelling at me or calling me names.

"Angela Lynn Carter! Do not force me to tell you again!" She jerked off the blankets.

I shivered as the cold morning air blew through the crack in the windowsill. I sat up and slid my legs under the blanket, making sure Mama didn't see. As the warmth of the blankets began to chase away the cold, I stretched my arms above my head, yawned, and rubbed the sleep from my eyes. When I removed my hands, I caught a glimpse of Mama leaving the room and pulling the door shut behind her. Mama, whose real name is Margret, tended to get angry over the least little thing. It didn't matter who or what upset her. I was the main target of her anger. She never took it out on me in front of Grandma. She waited until Grandma was in the garden or visiting friends.

I could hear Mama humming a tune as she moved about the kitchen. I was sleepy and could hardly keep my eyes open, so I lay back down, hoping to catch a few more winks. But then the humming stopped. I strained to listen. *Oh, no! She's coming!* I pulled the blankets over my head and lay exceptionally still, wondering what she was up to now. My heart raced as the sound of her footsteps drew nearer. She walked into the room, opened the curtains, and stood quietly. I lay paralyzed in fear. Waiting. Afraid to move. Afraid to breathe. Afraid of what was coming next.

Slowly pushing the blankets down, I peeked over them to see what she was doing. She stood with her back turned, looking out the window. The black dress that covered her three-hundred-fifty pounds hung just below her knees, and the size of her blocked most of the light from the window, making her appear even bigger and scarier than ever. She reminded me of one of those black demonic figures from the movies she always watched. She loved anything to do with the paranormal.

She stepped away from the window and began tidying up. I watched as dust particles danced in the golden rays of sunlight streaming into the room. *Oh no,* I thought. *What if Mama sees it?*

I tried to get her attention on something else before she saw it. But it was too late. She stormed out of the room and came back holding Daddy's belt. She grabbed me by my hair, yanked me out of bed, and beat me with it. The more I screamed and cried, the harder she hit me. "It's for your own good!" she yelled. "You're almost seven years old, Angela. Time to grow up!" At one point during the beating, I sat down on the floor, trying to keep the belt from hitting my legs. But instead, it wrapped around my face and busted my nose. I had never seen her that mad.

"You better not get blood on anything!" she yelled.

With both hands, I covered my nose, but as hard as I tried, I couldn't stop the bleeding. It ran down my chin and onto the front of my nightgown. I had blood all over my hands and face. Mama, in a fit of rage, wrapped her hands around my long blond hair once again and flung me across the room toward the window. I threw my hands out in front of me as I hit the wall, getting blood all over it. I quickly sat up, pressing my back against the wall.

"Look at the mess you made!" she screamed, then picked something up and threw it at me. It missed and hit the corner of the window, cracking it.

"Now look what you made me do!" she yelled, shaking with anger.

"I'm sorry, Mama."

"Get up and come here!" She pointed to the floor in front of her.

"What are you going to do?" I asked, not budging.

"I am going to lock you in the closet with the Boogeyman. He loves the blood of little girls," she said with a grin. "That will teach you."

"Please, Mama," I pleaded. "I'll do better. I promise I'll be good."

"I'll do better, Mama; I'll be good, Mama," she mocked. "But things never seem to get any better, do they, Angela? Now, we can do this the easy way or the hard way. It's up to you."

"No, Mama! Please don't put me in there," I pleaded.

"Okay, you asked for it, you little brat," she said.

She grabbed my arm and dragged me, kicking and screaming, across the floor to the closet. She struggled with the door. As soon as she opened it, I'd kick it shut, all the while pleading with her not to put me in there. I promised to be good. The more I begged, the harder she laughed. She finally got the door open, picked me up, and threw me in. My mind was made up; I wasn't going in there without a fight. Sticking my feet against the door frame, I kicked backward, hard, causing her to stumble, and we both hit the floor. She landed flat on her back, with me on top of her. She grabbed my hair, ripping some out as I rolled off and sat staring at her, unsure of what to do next.

She began rocking back and forth, struggling to get up. After several tries, she managed to roll to her side, and then upon her knees. While leaning against the bed, she took a few moments to catch her breath before pushing herself up onto one foot, and then the other. I knew I was in big trouble now. She was blocking my only way out. I scooted into the corner, curled into a ball and lay with my arms around my head, shaking with fear, and awaited the first blow. By then she had regained her composure and stood, looming over me like a giant grizzly bear.

Strands of my blond hair dangled from one hand, and daddy's belt in the other. She didn't see Grandma walk into the room. Just as Mama swung to hit me, Grandma grabbed the belt from her.

"Margret! That's enough!" she yelled.

"What are you going to do about it, you old hag?" she shouted, lifting me off the floor by one arm.

Grandma's face grew ghostly white as she looked at me. "Oh, Lord," she gasped, placing her hand over her mouth. "Margret, what have you done?" She ran toward me, but Mama blocked her way, knocking me down in the process.

"Move out of my way!" shouted Grandma, her face red with anger. She tried shoving her out of the way, but Grandma's one-hundred-thirty-pound frame was no match for Mama. Stepping back, with tears streaming down her face, she turned and ran out of the room.

I looked on in stunned silence before crying out, "Help me, Grandma! Please don't leave me!"

It was too late; she had already gone. I felt as though all hope was lost. The only one who could help me had left me.

Mama turned her attention back to me and grinned teasingly. "Look at poor pathetic little Angela, lying on the floor, crying like a baby." She ranted and raved for several minutes, but I managed to block out most of it.

"Your grandma can't help you, Angela. She has abandoned you." She smiled.

Suddenly her smile turned to a look of pain. I thought she was having fits, as she began jumping and squealing like a pig. With my back against the wall, I quickly moved out of her way and crouched in the corner.

It was then I saw what had caused all the commotion. There stood Grandma, holding a switch. She must have broken it off one of the trees out back.

"How does it feel, Margret?" Grandma asked as she struck Mama across her bare legs.

I never saw my mother's fat legs move so fast as she danced, jumped, and screamed trying to get away. Seeing my chance, I scrambled to my feet, and then ran and hid behind Grandma. She motioned for me to get out of the room. "Angel, go to the bathroom. I'll be there in a minute."

Without a word, I ran to the bathroom and closed the door. I climbed into the tub and hid behind the shower curtain. I sat there with my hands over my ears, silently crying and praying that God would protect us both.

"Mother, look at what you did to my legs! They are covered in welts," Mama yelled. Only this time she was the one crying like a baby. My heart ached for her. I didn't want anyone, not even Mama, to feel that kind of pain. Yet, at the same time, I was glad she was the one on the receiving end for a change.

"Now you know how that child feels," Grandma said. "You weren't raised that way, Margret. When you were growing up, your father and I did not so much as spank you. Maybe that's where we went wrong," she said sadly.

She looked around the room. "Where did you hide the phone?"

"Why? What are you going to do?" Mama moved to the living room.

"I'm going to call an ambulance," Grandma replied.

"I don't need an ambulance," Mama said.

"Well, that's good, because it's not for you!" Grandma said sarcastically. "Angel needs to be checked out to make sure nothing is broken."

"No! You're not calling anyone. She's fine." Mama tried to block the way. "And stop calling her *Angel*. Her name is *Angela*."

"If you don't call an ambulance, I will drive her to the hospital myself," Grandma said, ignoring Mama's last remark.

She took a few steps toward the bathroom, pausing before opening the door. "You better pray she's all right."

"Whatever!" Mama replied.

I could picture her rolling her eyes the way she always did when she disagreed with something Grandma was saying. I rolled my eyes once when I didn't like what Mama said, only to have her threaten to slap them out of my head if she ever caught me again. I never did—at least, not in front of her.

CHAPTER 2

GRANDMA TAKES CHARGE

I sat in the tub rocking back and forth for what seemed like an eternity. My knees were drawn to my chest with my arms wrapped around them. Every muscle in my body tightened upon hearing the bathroom door opening. I breathed a sigh of relief upon hearing Grandma say in a soft, gentle voice, "Angel, it's all right, honey. It's just me. You can come out now."

I peeked around the shower curtain before climbing out of the tub. I wrapped my arms around Grandma's waist and hugged her tight. She stood there for a moment stroking my hair, which was matted with blood. My heart leaped into my throat when I looked up and saw Mama standing in the doorway.

"Oh my God! What have I done?" Mama dropped to her knees and sobbed. She tried pulling me to her, but I stiffened, turned my head, and refused to look at her.

"Angela, I am so sorry," she continued. "I don't know what came over me. I love you, baby. I promise this will never happen again. Please forgive me." She sobbed so loud I had a hard time understanding what she was saying, nor did I care at that moment.

I was relieved when Grandma intervened. "Margret, I need to have a word with you in the other room."

Mama nodded, stood, and followed her. Several moments later, Grandma returned, alone.

I threw my arms around her and cried.

"Okay, baby," she said, taking hold of my arms and loosening my grip. "Time to get you cleaned up."

She ran the bath water while I undressed and tossed my bloody gown in the hamper.

Looking in the mirror, I saw my face covered in blood; there was a massive welt on one side of my face and halfway across the other. My hair was a tangled mess. I tried combing it with my fingers, but it was no use. I realized I had a sore spot on the right side of my head. I ran my fingers through my hair, trying to pinpoint exactly where the place was. I found what felt like a huge bump. Looking closely in the mirror, I cried when I saw blood slowly oozing from a hole in the center of it.

"Grandma, my head is bleeding!" I cried.

"It's all right. Just calm down while I take a look," she said in a soothing voice while searching through my hair. "There it is.

It's just a small gash, so don't you worry. How did that happen?"

I thought for a moment before answering. "I don't know. I don't remember hitting my head."

"Well, you can bet this will never happen again, not as long as I live," she said, placing a hand on each cheek and looking me in the eyes. And I knew she meant it.

She gently picked me up and set me in the tub. I closed my eyes and pictured a better life, a life without pain or worry, a life with just me and Grandma.

The warm water swirling around my legs seemed to ease the pain. Grandma lathered a washcloth with a bar of soap and gently washed away the blood. The soap stung in places I didn't know I'd been hit. I sat quietly while she finished bathing me and washing my hair. She pulled the plug.

I watched as the blood-stained water ran down the drain. She turned on the shower and told me to stand under the running water for a quick final rinse. I covered my face with my hands and leaned my head forward to keep the water out of my eyes and from raining down on the gash on top of my head. I was relieved when it was finally over.

Grandma wrapped a towel around me, and then lifted me from the tub. The warmth and softness of the cloth felt good on my battered and bruised little body. The welts on my back, legs, and face still stung, but felt better than they had.

Upon noticing the house seemed quieter than usual, I asked where Mama was.

"She'll be back later. I sent her to town for a few things." She picked me up, carried me to her room, and laid me on her bed, then stood staring at the floor for a moment before asking, "Can you tell me what happened?"

"I, uh, dust." I stammered. "There was dust on my dresser, but just a little."

"Oh, my word!" she exclaimed. "Did she beat you for that?"

"Well, I got blood on the wall when she threw me, but I didn't mean to. Then I made her break the window when she threw something at me, and I'm so sorry, Grandma. I tried to be good," I said, bursting into tears. "I promise, I tried."

"Angel, hun, listen to me." She sat by me on the bed and then picked me up and placed me on her lap. "You did nothing wrong; your Mama is the one who was wrong. I don't know what's going on with her. But I promise I'm going to find out. At the moment, all we can do is pray for her and let God take care of the rest."

"Okay, Grandma, I'll try. I will pray for her before I go to sleep tonight. But could you keep the switch in your room just in case?"

"I sure will." She laughed.

"Boy, you whipped her good, didn't you?" I said with a grin.

"That I did," she said, then added in a more serious tone, "I want you to remember that violence is never the answer. Don't ever think it's okay to abuse another person. It's not right in the eyes of God, nor in the eyes of the law. I only did what I had to do to stop her. I'm not proud of it, but I'd do it again in a heartbeat, given the same situation. I had a long talk with your mama, and she knows where I stand and what I will do should this ever happen again. I'm going to try to get her some help. Everything is going to be all right."

She laid me back on the bed and told me to stay put while she found me something to wear. I buried my face in the huge bath towel, waiting and praying the pain would go away.

I loved Grandma's room. It was bright and cheerful. I always felt safe and secure there, like nothing or no one could ever harm me.

I lay there as still as I could. I noticed that if I didn't move, the pain seemed to ease.

I was lost in thought and didn't hear Grandma come back into the room. She startled me when she spoke.

"I searched your room, but couldn't find anything," she said. "At least nothing nice, that is."

She must have noticed how tense I was. She smiled and kissed my forehead. "It's okay, sweetie. You're safe here with me. Everything is going to be just fine. Things are going to be different from now on. Now, cheer up, because I have a surprise for you."

"A surprise! Just for me?" She now had my full attention. "What is it?" I asked, trying to sit up, only to find it too painful.

"Now, now, you just lay still," she said, patting me gently on the arm. She got up and walked across the room to the closet.

"I was going to save it for your birthday next month, but now is as good a time as any." She held up a lavender colored dress. It was sleeveless, with a black velvet sash around the waist that tied in the back. In the front center of the sash was a diamond studded heart. The skirt, full of ruffles and lace, flared out.

"Wow!" I gritted my teeth through the pain and managed to get out of bed. "That is the prettiest dress I've ever seen. I love it," I said, holding it against me. "It's a princess dress. Can I try it on?"

"You sure can." She took the dress and then carefully slipped it over my head. "Well, now, would you look at that? It's a perfect fit."

"Thank you! Thank you! Thank you! I love it," I said, trying to jump up and down, which turned out to be more of a light bounce as I hugged her. "Now I look just like a princess!" I danced, twisted and twirled in my new dress. I loved the way it flared out and twirled as I spun around in circles. "Where did you get it?" I asked, admiring myself in the mirror.

"I made it especially for you," she answered.

"You make beautiful stuff, Grandma," I said, still twirling.

"I'm glad you like it. How would you like a bunch of dresses in all your favorite colors?" Grandma asked. "Well, maybe not as frilly as this one, but they will be just as lovely."

"I would love that," I said, wrapping my arms around her waist. "I love you so much, Grandma."

"I love you, too, my little Angel. I have another surprise for you."

"Another one? What is it?" I asked.

"You'll see." She smiled.

She opened the closet and pulled a blanket off the top shelf.

"Here, take this," she said, handing it to me. "Go out back and spread it on the ground underneath the big maple tree and wait for me there."

"Okie-dokie." I took the blanket and ran through the living room and into the kitchen. I paused at the back door and peered out the window before opening it. It was a perfect day for a picnic.

CHAPTER 3

THE PICNIC

Once outside, I stood for a moment, taking in the beauty all around me, from the little purple violas growing in the yard to the yellow dandelions Mama hated so much. Everything was peaceful. The flowers and grass swayed back and forth as if dancing to music only they could hear. The warm, gentle breeze felt wonderful as it blew through my hair.

The sun peeped out from behind huge, puffy white clouds as they slowly drifted past. I leaned my head back and smiled as the warmth of sunlight kissed my face. Two birds playfully chased one another, soaring across the sky, then stretching out their wings and gracefully gliding on the air. I listened as others chirped somewhere in the trees as if cheering them on. I couldn't help but wonder what it would be like to be a bird, flying through the sky, floating on the wings of the wind, happy and carefree.

I made my way to the big maple tree, spread the blanket on the ground beneath it, and then lay down and waited for Grandma. When she appeared a few minutes later, her hands full, I ran to help. She handed me two cartons of milk, and she carried the rest.

"Are we having a picnic?" I asked.

"We sure are," she said with a smile. She placed her Bible and the bagged lunch in the center of the blanket, then pulled two paper plates out of the bag, handed one to me and put the other on her lap. Next were two ham and cheese sandwiches wrapped in foil, two small bags of potato chips, and a mixed fruit cup. She placed everything on our plates.

I asked if I could say grace.

She nodded.

So, with heads bowed, eyes closed, and hands folded, I prayed a simple prayer Grandma had taught me: "God is great, God is good, and we thank Him for our food. By His hands we all are fed, Give us, Lord, our Daily Bread. Amen." It had started out as a horrible morning, but it was turning into a beautiful day. I thanked Grandma for the delicious meal. She informed me it wasn't over yet. Reaching into the bag and pulling out two chocolate chip cookies, she handed one to me. I slowly nibbled at it, savoring every bite until it was gone, and then drank the rest of the milk.

After lunch was over, we threw the trash in the bag and then lay on the blanket. My belly was full, and I felt comfortable and at peace.

Grandma told Bible stories. We sang silly songs, looked for shapes in the clouds, and then she taught me how to pray for others. As the day wound down, we lay in silence for what seemed like hours. I was taking it all in—I loved to feel the warm summer breeze as it blew through my hair and over my legs. Everything felt so tranquil, just the two of us lying there, listening to the rustling of the leaves as the wind gently blew through the trees. Birds were singing and chipmunks were chattering.

An ant ran off with a breadcrumb it found on the blanket. It struggled as it made its way through the grass around pebbles and twigs until it finally reached its home, a hole in the ground surrounded by sand. I watched in amazement as it dropped the crumb at the opening and went down the tunnel, only to reappear a second later to retrieve its prize. It pulled and wriggled until it finally managed to get it down the hole.

"I love this day." I rolled onto my side and propped my head up with my hand. I told Grandma about the dreams I'd been having of a beautiful lady in a long flowing white gown.

"Perhaps the lady in your dreams is your guardian angel."

I thought for a moment, sat up and said, "I think God truly does love me, because he sent me two guardian angels."

"I thought there was only one in your dream," she said.

"There was, silly." I giggled. "You are my other one."

"Oh, my." Grandma pulled me into her arms and hugged me tightly. Tears welled in her eyes. "I do believe that is the sweetest thing I have ever heard." Pulling a tissue from her pocket, she dabbed at the tears just before they rolled down her cheek. She looked at me with such sadness. "I am so sorry, little one. I should have recognized all the signs of abuse. I'm so mad I could kick myself for not seeing it earlier, but I promise you from here on out, I will always guard and protect you the best I can. And I want you to promise me that if your Mama ever hurts you again, you will tell me."

"I promise I will tell you from now on," I said.

"I just can't for the life of me understand how she can do that to her only child. And, what's worse, is why I didn't know it," she said softly, crying.

"Don't cry, Grandma. You didn't know because Mama only did it when you were out of the house, like when you were in the garden or with the ladies on bridge night. I didn't tell you because Mama said she would whip me twice as hard if I did."

"Well, I won't be going out anymore unless you're with me. No more bridge nights on Tuesdays or quilting nights on Thursdays. And when I'm in the garden, I will take you with me. You can play until I get through." She patted my arm. "There now, it's all settled. I will keep you safe by keeping you away from her as much as possible. Does that sound all right to you?"

"No, Grandma, it's not all right. You love spending time with your friends, playing cards and sewing. We can pray for Mama as you said, and God will watch over both of us."

Grandma smiled sweetly. "Little one, you are wise beyond your years. You've always been my little Angel and always will be."

CHAPTER 4

SEVENTH BIRTHDAY

Grandma kept her word. A few weeks passed and she never let me out of her sight. I played in her room while she busied herself sewing. She made several new dresses for me in a rainbow of colors. When we weren't in her room, we did yard work. I helped rake leaves, which we used to make a scarecrow by stuffing an old pair of pants and shirt that I had outgrown.

We placed it in the front yard along with a few other Halloween decorations we made. I'm not sure which one of us enjoyed it more. I wished someone besides the three of us could see what a great job we did, which was unlikely since we never got trick or treaters, let alone visitors, there on Primrose Mountain, West Virginia.

The mountain got its name from the abundance of primroses—of all colors—that grew along the roadside. We lived at the very top of the mountain in a two-story farmhouse.

Our closest neighbor was Old Man Sims, who lived about a half mile down the road. Sometimes I heard his dogs barking. He must've had a dozen of them. Some he used for hunting; others were strays he took in. He was always rescuing animals, especially dogs. Maybe Grandma could talk him into coming to see our decorations. According to her, he was a loving man with a kind heart. But Mama described him much differently, so I wasn't sure who to believe. Mama said with his scraggly beard, uncombed hair, dirty bibbed overalls and bad teeth, he had poor personal hygiene. I'm not sure what that meant, but if you ask me, I think he needed a bath.

Grandma said his house could use a woman's touch, and that it looked as bad and unkempt as he did. He had all kinds of junk piled everywhere. The house itself was in severe need of repair and could use a good coat of paint.

Our home was white with black shutters. A huge porch stretched across the entire front of the house, wrapping around the right side. A swing hung at the end of the porch, a purple rhododendron bush grew next to the steps, and maple trees Daddy had planted before I was born lined the long dirt driveway leading to the meticulous yard. Daddy had been a coal miner. He also owned his own landscaping business, which he and Mama ran on weekends.

I don't remember Daddy; he died a few days after my first birthday. I know he loved me very much. Grandma said I was the apple of his eye. I never understood what that meant, but I knew it must be good. Mama took his death hard, and according to Grandma, she wasn't the same since. Sometimes I wondered how different life would have been if he'd lived.

It was an exceptionally warm night. The moon shined brightly in the sky. I climbed into bed, pulled the covers over me, and lay there reflecting on the events of the day. I smiled and folded my hands in prayer. "God, please let everyday be like today." Feeling content, I rolled over and drifted off to sleep.

Morning came much too soon, the sunlight relentless in its intensity shined brightly through the window, settling across my bed. I lazily rolled over and opened first one eye and then the other. I sat up and dangled my legs over the side of the bed, and stared sleepily at the floor. I was unusually tired this morning. I forced myself to get up when all I really wanted was lay back down and pull the blankets over my head.

I heard a light knock on the door and was surprised when Grandma walked in holding a beautifully wrapped gift. She handed it to me.

"Happy birthday day!" she shouted.

I had forgotten what day it was. I sat back on the bed and quickly opened it. I was thrilled to see several bottles of nail polish, a bracelet with dangling kittens, puppies and colored jewels, and a jewelry box to keep it in.

"Thank you, I love them all." I hugged her tight.

"I was hoping you would like them." She grinned.

Mama peeked in the room. "May I come in?"

"Yes, ma'am." I scrambled off the bed. "Look at my birthday gift from Grandma." I held up the box for her to see.

"Those are lovely." Mama smiled. "I have a gift for you as well. Would you like it now or later?"

"Now, please." I could hardly contain my excitement. I don't remember Mama ever buying me a birthday gift.

"Here ya go." She pulled a gift bag from behind her back and handed it to me. She stood smiling, awaiting my reaction.

I opened it and squealed with delight. It was a new cowgirl outfit, boots, and matching hat.

"Oh, my goodness, they are beautiful. Thank you so much, Mama." I hugged her, and she leaned down and kissed the top of my head.

I pulled the jeans from the box and slipped them on, and then the boots and shirt. I loved the way the fringes dangled from the shoulders and down the sleeves. I handed Grandma the bracelet and she fastened it around my wrist.

"Oh my, you look very pretty." Grandma took my hand and spun me around in circles.

"You make a beautiful cowgirl," Mama said. She stepped back toward the door and paused. "Mother, I need to run into town for a few things. Would you mind watching Angela until I get back?"

~ 32 ~

"Um, no. I don't mind at all," Grandma said, a confused look crossed her brow.

I understood Grandma's confusion. Mama had never asked her to babysit me before. She usually left without a word.

"Aren't you going to have breakfast first?" Grandma asked.

"No, thanks. I'm just going to the library to read up on a few things. I'll grab something in town." Mama turned and hurried out the door.

After breakfast, Grandma immersed herself in sewing, while I busied myself with homeschool work and painting my nails. I held up my hands to show Grandma.

"Oh, my, they look pretty," she said.

"Maybe I can paint yours after lunch." I grinned.

"My goodness, is it lunch time already?" Grandma said. "Well, in that case, I am done for the day." She stood and stretched.

"What's for lunch?" I asked.

"How does a sandwich and a glass of chocolate milk sound?" She winked.

"Sounds good to me." My stomach growled in agreement.

"Would you like to carve a pumpkin after lunch?" she asked.

"I have never carved a pumpkin before," I answered.

"Well, that's because you were too young, but now that you're an old woman— how old are you, twenty-five?" she teased.

"No, Grandma, I'm seven." I giggled

"Great. You're old enough." She smiled, took my hand, and led me to the kitchen. There, on the table, sat the biggest pumpkin I'd ever seen.

"Wow! Where did that come from?" I asked.

"I picked it out of the garden this morning," she said proudly.

"Wow! It was small when I saw it last." I patted the pumpkin. "I thought you bought it."

"No need buying something you can grow yourself," she said.

"Can I grow one?" I asked.

"I have an even better idea," she said excitedly. "When spring arrives, you can plant your very own garden—much smaller, of course."

"That would be awesome!" I said enthusiastically. I now had something to look forward to.

After lunch, we began carving the pumpkin. I enjoyed scooping out the insides, which would later be used to make pies. After roasting the seeds, we worked on the face. Grandma carved the mouth, then I helped with the eyes. Afterward, she placed a candle inside.

"There, now. This is what you call a jack o'lantern," she said, admiring our work.

"I think it looks wonderful." I stepped back for a better view. "What are we going to do with it?"

"Let's set it on the front porch." Grandma picked it up, while I ran ahead and held the door open. We stepped outside and were shocked to find a huge dog standing in the yard. He had torn the leg off the scarecrow. It still hung from his mouth, and he began shaking it vigorously. Leaves flew out of it.

"Get out of here!" Grandma shouted. She sat the jack o'lantern on the step, grabbed the broom and chased the dog off.

"Oh no, look what he has done," Grandma said sadly. "Maybe I can fix it."

"It's okay, Grandma. I have an idea." I picked it up, re-stuffed it with leaves, replaced the sock and shoe, and then shoved the end in the mouth of the jack o'lantern. "There. Now it looks like he came alive and tried to eat the scarecrow."

"That has got to be the funniest Halloween decoration I have ever seen." Grandma chuckled. She went inside to get her camera, and took lots of pictures of me with our finished project.

Mama returned home just in time to get in on the fun. She laughed when she saw the legless scarecrow and the jack o'lantern. "What a clever idea," she said.

Grandma took photos of Mama and me. Then I took a few of the two of them before Mama decided to take the bag of stuff she bought to her room.

"What'd you buy, Mama?" I questioned.

She paused at the foot of the stairs. " Oh, just a game," she answered over her shoulder.

"Can I play?" I asked.

"Maybe later." She winked, then rushed upstairs to her room.

I ran to the bathroom to clean up, while Grandma called Old Man Sims to talk to him about the dog.

"What did he say?" I asked.

"He said it wasn't one of his, but he would be right up to look for it."

"Yay!" I clapped my hands. "He can see our Halloween decorations."

Before long I heard the clattering of his old pickup truck coming up the road. The rhythmic pounding echoed through the hills. I stood on the front porch and watched him pull up our long driveway.

"Grandma, he's here!" I hollered.

"Coming!" she yelled.

I was so excited I ran down the steps to meet Old Man Sims. He parked his truck and barely had time to get out before I grabbed him by the hand.

"Come look at what we made," I said excitedly.

"Slow down, child. I ain't as young as I used to be." Old Man Sims laughed.

"See?" I pointed to the jack o'lantern. "He ate the scarecrow's leg."

"What in tarnation? I better run before he eats my leg." Old Man Sims pretended to run away.

I grabbed his hand. "It's okay. It's fake." I giggled.

"Are you sure?" he asked

"Yes, sir, I'm sure. The dog tore the scarecrow's leg off, and I put it in the jack o'lantern's mouth."

"Well, it sure scared the daylights out of me," Old man Sims said. "I believe that is the best decoration in all of West Virginia."

"Thank you," I said proudly.

Grandma stepped out onto the porch and overheard the whole conversation.

"That was Angel's idea." She smiled.

"Well, you have a bright little girl there," said Old Man Sims.

"You're not a crabby old man at all. I think you are a very nice man," I said.

"Angel! You apologize to Mr. Sims." Grandma's eyes landed on me.

"Did I say something wrong?" I asked.

"No. Not at all, little one," replied Old Man Sims. "As a matter of fact, I take that as a compliment." He laughed.

"Sorry about that," Grandma said, her face red.

"Virginia, I do believe red is a good color on you." Old Man Sims continued to laugh.

Grandma, at a loss for words, began wringing her hands, blushing all the more, causing Old Man Sims to laugh even harder. Grandma, unable to contain herself, joined him in laughter.

"Okay, I'll try to behave myself." Old Man Sims chuckled. "Now which way did that dog run off to?"

"He went that way." Grandma pointed toward the woods.

"Can I come with you?" I asked when Old Man Sims started walking toward the back of the house.

"I don't mind one bit, if it's all right with your Grandma," he replied.

"Can I, Grandma. Please?" I folded my hands in a begging gesture.

"Okay, I'll come with you." She took off her apron and laid it over the porch banister.

Old Man Sims stopped and waited for us to catch up. He grabbed my arm when I tried to run on ahead. "Hold it right there, kiddo." His expression serious.

"Why?" I asked.

"Because that dog may not be friendly." He smiled and rubbed my head.

We walked across the field, stopping at the edge of the woods. Old Man Sims began whistling for the dog, but we didn't see hide nor hair of him.

"Here, boy! Come out, come out, wherever you are," I shouted.

Everything was quiet except for the sound of frogs croaking somewhere in the field. All around us, crickets and bugs sang their evening song.

We were startled by an unexpected loud bark behind us, causing all three of us to jump. We turned, and there he stood—only he looked bigger than I had first thought.

"Harold! You big horse! What in tarnation are you doing up here bothering these people?" Old Man Sims stepped toward the dog with his hand outstretched.

The dog pounced forward with his head to the ground and his butt stuck up in the air, his tail wagging in a playful gesture.

"Harold! I don't have time for play". We all laughed in unison.

"Come here, Harold." I patted my leg.

Harold's ears perked up when he saw me. He bounded right toward me, knocking me to the ground. He began licking my face. I didn't have much time to react before Old Man Sims grabbed him and pulled him off me. "Settle down, Harold, ya big lug."

Grandma giggled and helped me to my feet. "It looks like you made a new friend." "I am sorry about that, kiddo," Old Man Sims said.

"It's all right. He just wanted to play." I laughed.

"She's fine," Grandma said. "And thank you for coming. It was an interesting evening." She chuckled.

We walked Old Man Sims and Harold to his truck and waved him off.

"I like them." I smiled up at Grandma.

"Me, too," Grandma said. "But now it's time we get busy baking."

We washed our hands in the bathroom. Grandma brushed leaves out of my hair. "Harold got me dirty, and I was covered in dog hair." I stretched out my shirt to show her.

"You go change while I get everything ready in the kitchen." She laughed and kissed the top of my head.

I ran to my room and quickly changed into a pair of dark blue sweatpants and a white tee-shirt.

Afterwards, I met Grandma in the kitchen. She handed me a mixing bowl. I helped her mix the batter for my birthday cake, and she helped me pour it into the cake pans. As it baked, the house filled with the sweet aroma of chocolate. Once done, Grandma removed it from the oven and placed it on top of the stove.

"Now, we'll make the frosting while the cake cools." She smiled and set a bowl on the table, along with a box of confectioners' sugar, butter, milk and cocoa. "There's nothing like homemade chocolate cake and frosting."

She measured the ingredients and I poured it in the bowl and stirred it. Mama joined us in the kitchen and sat quietly at the end of table.

"Hi, Mama. We're making frosting. Do you wanna taste it?" I asked, handing her a spoonful.

"Thank you, sweetie." She smiled and placed the tip of the spoon to her lips. "Yum, that's delicious."

"That's not how you eat frosting, silly." I giggled.

She handed me the spoon. "Then why don't you show me how it's done." She smiled and gave Grandma a little wink.

"Okay, open your mouth and stick out your tongue." I giggled.

I intended on holding the spoon up and swiping it over her tongue, but for whatever reason, she looked down and I

Williams

accidentally slid it over the end of her nose. Shocked, I took a step back. Before I had a chance to say anything, Mama grinned, and then stuck her finger in the frosting bowl and rubbed it down the length of my nose and chin.

Grandma burst into laughter. Mama and I looked at each other. A mischievous smile spread across our faces. We read each other's minds.

Grandma must have, too. She set the bowl of frosting on the counter and slowly backed away. "Don't even think about it," she said, shaking her finger at us.

"Let's get her!" shouted Mama.

We chased Grandma around the kitchen, and when we caught her, we held her down and rubbed her face full of frosting. The three of us lay there on the kitchen floor, laughing hysterically.

Grandma placed her hand on her stomach. "Oh goodness, my sides hurt." She took a deep breath and exhaled.

"I haven't laughed like that in a long time," Mama said. She stood, then helped Grandma up.

"That was fun." I took ahold of Mama's outstretched hand. She pulled me to my feet and kissed my forehead.

"You taste delicious." She giggled. "Guess we better clean up."

"Yes, you're right, and I need to make more frosting for the cake." Grandma laughed and threw a dishtowel at Mama as she walked past. We had a terrific evening. For once, we were a normal, loving family.

CHAPTER 5

THE BOOK

Several months passed without incident. I thought things were looking up. I was wrong.

Mama became distant. She spent most of her time at the library or upstairs in her room. Sometimes I heard her grumbling to herself or yelling at someone. Grandma said she must have been talking on the phone, but I don't think she believed that any more than I did. I heard voices, but Grandma said she heard nothing.

I longed for the loving mother she had been a few months before. At least she hadn't laid a finger on me since Grandma had a talk with her.

I wanted to spend time with Mama when I caught her in a better mood, which these days were few and far between. One minute she was sweet, and the next she was angry. This morning she was quiet and kept to herself.

I had just gotten out of the shower when I heard a tap on the bathroom door.

"Angela, are you in there?" Mama asked.

"Yes, ma'am."

"I have to run into town to return a book at the library," she yelled through the door. "Don't disturb your grandma. She isn't feeling well."

"Okay, Mama."

"I'll leave you some milk and cookies on the kitchen table," she said sweetly. "I love you."

"Thank you. I love you too."

I wanted to jump for joy. Mama was back to her old self. But a bad feeling came over me. Something awful was about to happen, I just knew it. I never told anyone, but I'd had this feeling before, and it always proved true and it always involved Mama. I shivered at the thought.

I took my time getting dressed and stayed in the bathroom until I heard the front door open and close. I walked into the living room and peered out the window. I breathed a sigh of relief when I saw her pull out of the driveway.

I tiptoed to Grandma's room. The door was slightly ajar. I pushed it open enough to peek in. She was sleeping soundly. I pulled the door shut and quietly tiptoed across the living room.

I went to the kitchen and found the glass of milk and cookies on the table just as Mama had said. I pulled out a chair and was about sit down when I noticed a book laying on the counter. I walked over and picked it up. It was black and tattered with a strange symbol on the cover—a star with a circle around it. The title was "The Power of Witchcraft." I opened it and flipped through it, stopping on a page that had a creepy picture of a devil with huge horns and piercing red eyes that seemed to stare right through me. I tried looking away, but I couldn't. Its evil gaze had me transfixed. It was as though an invisible force held me like a magnet on metal. I felt strange and lightheaded, even queasy.

A male voice softly whispered my name. "Angela, join us, Angela. We can give you power to do great things."

"No! I can't," I whispered.

"Come on, Angela. You know you want to. Join us and we'll get rid of your mother. She will never bother you again." It laughed, a deep menacing laugh.

I could feel evilness all around me. The voice grew louder and angrier when I fought it.

"No!" I whispered.

"Join us or die, you little bitch!" it shouted, which sounded more like a growl.

Just then I heard a woman's voice, loud and clear. I recognized her—she was the one from my dreams. "Angel, resist them. You are stronger than they are." Her voice was so gentle and soothing, yet over-powered the others.

A song my grandmother used to sing to me played in my mind. *Jesus loves me.* The song grew louder in my head. I realized I was singing it aloud over and over until the force that held me released its grip. My legs buckled and I fell to the floor. After a few moments, I stood, looked around the room dumbfounded, trying to wrap my head around what had just happened. The book still lay open on the counter. I refused to look at it.

I heard a car door slam, then footsteps on the front porch. I closed the book and ran back to the table and took a seat.

The door opened and Mama hurried into the kitchen. She paused, glancing from me to the book on the counter. She rushed over, grabbed it, and held it to her chest. I dunked a cookie in the milk and pretended not to notice.

"Did you forget something?" I asked nonchalantly.

"Huh? Um, yes, I forgot my book." She stared at me, still clutching it tightly.

I placed the glass of milk to my lips and took a huge gulp.

"Angela, did you—"

"What mama?" I asked, pretending to be preoccupied with my snack.

"Never mind." She shook her head, then turned to leave.

I ran after her. "Mama, wait! I have something to tell you."

She spun around facing me. "Yes, what is it?"

Before I had a chance to answer, the glass I was drinking from flew off the table and landed on the floor behind me. It shattered, spilling what was left of the milk all over the floor.

From the look on her face, she was as shocked as I was. She nervously fidgeted with her car keys. "Uh, I, uh," she stuttered, her eyes scanning the living room.

"You feel it, too, don't you, Mama?" I asked.

"What are you talking about?" She grabbed my shoulders and shook me. "Did you read the book? Answer me!" she shouted.

"No, Mama, I didn't read anything." I wasn't lying, but now I was afraid to tell her what really happened.

"It's just a book about scary stories," she lied. "I am taking it back to the library so there is no need to mention it to your grandma. Is that clear?" she asked.

"Yes, ma'am." I stooped down to pick up the broken glass.

"Leave it. I'll clean it up when I get back." She opened the front door and paused. "Wait in your room until I get home. I won't be long."

"I'm scared. Can I come with you?" I asked, on the verge of tears.

"It's okay, you must have set the glass too close to the edge of the table and it simply fell off. I need you to stay here and keep an eye on your grandma. Everything is going to be all right. I promise." She kissed my forehead and left me standing there alone and scared.

I ran to my room, locked the door, and prayed for God to protect us all.

Later that night, I got up to use the bathroom. On the way back to bed, I saw Mama walking toward the kitchen talking to herself. I thought I heard male voices whispering, but no one was there. I wanted to believe it was my imagination, but after what happened earlier, I wasn't so sure. I waited for Mama to go back upstairs, then tiptoed to Grandma's room. Her bedside lamp was on and she woke when she heard the door shut behind me.

"It's just me, Grandma," I whispered. "How are you feeling?"

"Not so good, baby," she answered. "Is everything all right?"

"No it's not. I heard voices, but no one was there," I blurted out without thinking.

"You probably had a bad dream, that's all." She tried to sit up, but sank back into her pillow.

"I have a horrible headache," she said. "Would you hand me a couple acetaminophen, and the bottle of water there on the nightstand?"

"Here you go." I placed the medicine in her hand, opened the bottle of water, and handed it to her.

"Thank you, darlin'." She placed the pills in her mouth and washed them down with the water.

"Grandma, I need to tell you about the voices." I nervously looked around her room.

"It's late, sweetie, and we both need to get some sleep. We can talk about your dream in the morning."

I wanted to tell her it wasn't a dream, but instead I kissed her cheek and turned to leave.

"Goodnight, I love you," she whispered.

"I love you too. Goodnight."

I went back to my room and climbed into bed, but sleep didn't come easy. Every time I closed my eyes, I saw the creepy picture from the book. I tossed and turned for what felt like hours. Finally, after a few prayers, I drifted off to sleep and once again dreamed of the beautiful lady, my Guardian Angel.

Three days passed, and Grandma hadn't gotten any better. The day before, she asked Mama to take her to the hospital, but her plea was ignored. She was sleeping a lot and I was terribly worried. Her breakfast and lunch went untouched. Hopefully, she would eat something later.

Later that evening, Mama was in the kitchen making dinner and mumbling to herself. I walked in, hoping to convince her to take Grandma to see a doctor. She stood by the table, her back turned. I walked up behind her and was about to speak when she place her hands on each side of her head, covering her ears, "Go away. Leave me alone," she whispered.

Is she talking to me? I wondered.

"Mama, are you all right?"

No response. I stepped closer and placed a hand on her shoulder. "Mama," I whispered.

Her hands dropped to her side. "Go to your room," she said calmly.

"Grandma needs to see a doctor. She's—"

She glanced at me over her shoulder. For a split second, her eyes flashed black, then went back to normal.

"I said, go to you room. Now!" she shouted.

Frightened, I ran to my room and stayed there the rest of the evening, hoping and praying Grandma would be all right. Questions whirled through my mind. *What is going on with Mama? Did I see what I thought I saw, or was it my imagination?* Questions I had no answers for, but maybe Grandma would know, if only she wasn't so sick. *Oh, God, how I needed her right now.*

Later that night, I sneaked into Grandma's room, She was sleeping, her breathing labored. I gently kissed her fevered

~ 51 ~

brow and then tiptoed back to my room. I got down on my knees and said a prayer for her before climbing into bed. I had trouble falling asleep due to hunger pangs. I had been sent to my room without dinner, and now I was feeling the effects of it.

CHAPTER 6

GRANDMA'S SICK

I awoke early to find Mama standing over me. The delicious aroma of fried bacon and buttered toast filled the air. I crossed my arms and pressed them against my stomach, trying to calm the hunger pangs. I had been sent to bed the night before without dinner. For what, I had no clue.

"Angela, I am talking to you." Mama snapped her fingers.

"Uh, sorry, Mama, I didn't hear you."

She leaned over and pointed her finger at my face. "I want you to hear me, and you listen well. I'm trying to be kind to you. Do not embarrass me or I will whip you like I did several months ago. Don't forget, your grandma is sick in bed, and she's in no shape to come to your rescue."

I shuddered at the thought of going through that again. Before leaving my room, Mama turned to me, then sweetly said,

"Angela, dear, come on, get up, everything is ready. You're having breakfast with me this morning."

I stared at her in disbelief. She never let me eat meals with her. I always had to wait and eat the leftovers, if there were any.

"What's the matter, girl?" Mama laughed. "You look like a deer caught in headlights. Now, come on, get up, and get dressed. I need you to be on your best behavior today. We may have a visitor."

"Who is coming to visit us, Mama?" I asked.

"A new friend I made while in town the other day." She smiled. "And guess what? She has a little girl the same age as you."

"Really?" I squealed with delight. "What's her name?"

"Yes, really. You can ask her when she gets here. Now, get dressed. We're going to have a beautiful day today."

"What should I wear?" I asked.

"Well, now, let's see," she said, rummaging through drawers and looking in the closet.

All my clothes were rags. If they weren't torn or stained, they were too small. I couldn't remember the last time, if ever, Mama had bought me something new.

"Wait, I know!" I said excitedly. "Can I please wear the new dress Grandma made me for my birthday?"

"Angela, that dress is long gone," Mama said. "Didn't you know your Grandma got rid of it?"

"No, Mama. She didn't. It's in her room."

"I thought I made it clear to the old hag to burn that dress," Mama said, her smile disappearing. "But no matter. Go get it if you can find it, put it on, and then come to breakfast." She began humming once again as she left the room.

I slid out of bed and straightened it as best I could, then ran to Grandma's room. Pausing at the door, I held my breath and listened for Mama. I breathed a sigh of relief upon hearing sounds coming from the kitchen. I slowly opened the door and then stepped in gently, closing it behind me.

I stood in the center of the room, looking around, unsure of what to do next. I jumped when Grandma stirred, letting out a low moan as she turned to face me. She smiled faintly upon seeing me standing there.

"Sorry, Grandma. I didn't mean to wake you," I said, pausing at her bedside. "Grandma, you aren't going to die, are you?"

She smiled sweetly and motioned for me to come closer. Taking my hand, she whispered, "Not if I can help it."

"What's wrong with you? Why are you so sick?" I asked. "I've been praying for you, but I don't think God is listening to me."

"Whoa, slow down, child. One question at a time." She held up her hand. "I'm pretty sure I have pneumonia, and that's why I'm so sick. I need you to keep praying, because God is listening, and He will answer your prayers as long as you have faith."

"What is faith?" I asked.

Scooting over to make room, she patted the bed, indicating that she wanted me to sit by her.

I climbed up and sat perfectly still, waiting for her to quit coughing. She coughed so hard and long, she had a hard time catching her breath.

Fear cut through me like a knife. "I'll get Mama," I said.

She placed her hand on my leg, shaking her head. The coughing finally subsided, and she settled back onto her pillow.

"Let me try to help you understand about faith," she said with a faint but proud smile. "The Bible says in Hebrews chapter eleven verse one, 'Now faith is the substance of things hoped for, the evidence of things not seen.' What that means is simply this—if you hope and believe in your heart that God is going to do something, and you ask it in Jesus's name, He will do it."

Leaning forward, I placed my hand on her fevered brow, closed my eyes, and prayed. "Dear God, please make my Grandma better real soon, and I believe you will, with all my heart. Oh, yeah! I almost forgot. In Jesus's name. Amen." I opened my eyes. "How was that?"

"That was perfect." She looked at me with tear-filled eyes. "Is that bacon I smell?" She looked toward the door.

I nodded and told her how different Mama was this morning, how she woke me up and said I could eat breakfast with her and wear my new birthday dress for the visitors.

"Visitors?" she asked with a look of concern in her eyes. She told me to be on my best behavior and not to do anything to upset Mama. I promised to be good. She revealed to me where the dress was hidden and told me not to tell Mama about her hiding spot. It felt good to share a secret hiding place with Grandma. I slipped into the dress and then kissed Grandma before leaving her room.

"Angel, honey would you bring me the phone?" Grandma asked, her voice weak.

"Would you like me to call someone for you?" I smiled.

"No, dear, I'll do it. I need to call an ambulance to take me to the hospital."

"Okay, I'll be right back." I ran into the living room but the phone wasn't on the charger. Mama must have left it in the kitchen.

CHAPTER 7

BREAKFAST WITH MAMA

I nervously walked into the kitchen. Mama never acknowledged I had entered the room. She sat at the table smoking a cigarette while reading a book . I stood, staring at the front cover. *Oh God! She still has it.* A chill ran down my spine. My breakfast was sitting at the end of the table. I dared not touch it, even though hunger pangs and my rumbling stomach seemed to beg me to take just one bite. After a few minutes, she slammed the book down, pushed herself back from the table, and stood glaring at me.

"What are you looking at, you filthy little tramp?" she shouted.

"Nothing," I whispered. "Grandma needs to call an ambulance."

"You spent so much time in the room with your grandma that you missed breakfast. Now your food is nasty and cold." She pointed at my plate, ignoring my last comment.

I quickly walked to the table, climbed upon the chair, and sat down. "That's okay, Mama. I don't mind."

I picked up a slice of bacon, but just as I opened my mouth to take a bite, she slapped it from my hand. She then grabbed my plate and dumped it in the pail of leftovers she'd later feed the dogs. We had four of them. They were pinned up out back; I wasn't allowed to go near them. Mama said they were vicious and would bite my arm off, but in my opinion, if anyone was mean, it was her. She was almost as cruel to them as she was to me. I say almost, because unlike me, they were fed every day. Since Grandma had been sick, I was lucky if I got a slice of bread, but that was something I kept to myself. I didn't want to upset her.

"After all the trouble I went through to make a nice meal, and you show up late and still expect to have breakfast with me. You're a disrespectful, hateful, little brat!" Mama shouted.

"You're the hateful brat!" I yelled back at her. I slid off the chair and stood there in stunned silence. I couldn't believe what had just came out of my mouth. I had never spoken to Mama like that, and from the look on her face, I knew I was in for it.

"Oh, hell no!" she shouted. "You know better than to talk to me like that."

I tried to run, but I wasn't quick enough. Mama grabbed me. She held her cigarette against my arm. Just as I screamed out in pain, she stuffed a dirty rag in my mouth. The smell of burning flesh mixed with tobacco made me sick. She dropped the cigarette, yanked my head back by my hair, and clenched her chubby fingers around my throat. I could feel them drawing tighter and tighter, cutting off the air as I so desperately fought to breathe. As I crumpled under her weight, I could feel myself passing out or dying—I'm not sure which. She had me pinned to the floor, and I couldn't move.

Releasing her grip, she slapped me hard across the face. "What were you thinking?" She shook me. "Answer me!"

I lay there coughing and gagging, trying to take in a deep breath of air. I finally managed to speak. "Food, Mama. I, I was hungry," I stuttered, choking back tears with little luck.

"You were hungry!" she mockingly said as she got up. She didn't take her eyes off me. She hovered over me like a cat stalking its prey. A look of pure evil filled her eyes as she glared down at me.

I managed to sit up. I hugged my knees tight against my chest. Finally, after what seemed like an eternity, she kicked me hard in the leg and shouted, "You'll eat when the dogs eat—if there's anything left." She walked over and threw my empty plate into the sink. I heard it shatter into what sounded like a thousand pieces. She sat back down at the table and began to finish her breakfast.

"Margret! You leave that child alone," Grandma shouted from the bedroom. She always took up for me, especially after she found out about the abuse. Most of the time, Mama backed off.

"Shut up, old woman, and mind your own business!" she yelled. She turned her attention back to me and said with a half grin, "Your grandma can't help you today, Angela. She's too sick to get out of bed."

"That's okay, Mama. I'm not hungry anymore." I stood. "I'll just go to my room now."

"You'll leave when I say you can go." She grabbed me by my hair and forced me to my knees. "Do you want food, Angela? Then beg for it." She laughed aloud.

Tears welled in my eyes. She must've seen them too. The smile left her face, and she stared at me through those piercing evil eyes that now appeared to have turned black. She then said through clenched teeth, "If you cry, you get nothing! Now beg."

I tried hard to choke back tears, and answered in a voice that was so tiny I almost didn't hear it. "Please, Mama."

"You call that begging?" she shouted. "You'll have to do better than that."

"Please, Mama," I said a little louder, my voice quivering. I could no longer hold back the tears. They streamed down my cheeks like a dam bursting forth.

"Margret!" Grandma shouted, banging her hand against the wall.

I looked up to see her standing in the doorway of the kitchen. Neither of us heard her get out of bed and make her way into the room.

"You weren't treated that way as a child, and I am not going to let you treat this child that way."

Mama slowly released the grip she had on my hair. She walked to the counter and grabbed a stale piece of bread from the dogs' feeding pail.

"Oh, Angela." She laughed aloud. "Do you have any idea how pathetic you look sitting there begging for food like a dog? If you're going to act like a dog, you might as well eat like one." The smile left her face and the look in her eyes cut right through me. She threw the bread on the floor in front of me. I barely had enough time to grab it before she grabbed me by the arm and dragged me to my room, and then shoved me down on the cold hard floor.

I crawled across the room and sat with my back to the wall.

Grandma tried to stop her, but it was no use. She began coughing again and could hardly catch her breath.

"Go to bed, Mother! I was only having a little fun with Angela."

"That is no way to treat your own flesh and blood," Grandma replied angrily. "I told you I would not stand for it. Either you get your act together, or I will be calling Child Protective Services. Angela will be removed from here, and you will go to jail."

"Calm down, Mother. I didn't hurt her; I was only teaching her a lesson."

"I mean it, Margret. I've had enough!" Grandma shouted as she turned and began making her way back to her room.

"All right, Mother! I hear you loud and clear," Mama yelled before turning her attention back to me. "I'm going to call my friend and tell her not to come today. See what you did? Because of you, my friend can't come to visit. Why do you always have to ruin everything?"

The anger rose in her voice as she began to rant once again. I managed to block out most of it by trying to imagine myself in a happier place. I thought of my dreams and the beautiful lady whom I now referred to as my guardian angel. That's what Grandma called her, and I liked the thought of having my very own guardian angel. I imagined her coming to save me from this horrible life and giving me a better one, even if it meant going to heaven and living with her there.

"You stay out of my sight!" Mama spit at me.

"Yes, ma'am," I replied.

I scooted to the corner and lay there curled up, silently praying she would just go away. For a minute, I thought she was going to start up again, but instead, she took a step back and turned to leave, locking the door behind her. She grumbled to herself as she made her way back to the kitchen.

She slammed dishes and cabinet doors, grumbling all the while about not letting such a disrespectful child get away with talking to her that way. The more she thought about it, the angrier she became. She began spewing profanities and throwing things. Glass shattered.

Grandma came to my room. "Angel, run. Run and hide."

I knew just where to go.

Grandma went back to the kitchen to try to calm Mama down while I made my escape. I opened my bedroom door and peeked out. They were arguing in the kitchen. I slowly stepped out, closing the door behind me. I ran through the living room and out the front door as fast as my little feet could carry me. I was a scrawny little thing, and I'll bet you could have counted every rib in my frail, bony little body.

I crept around the side of the house until I came to a loose board, which was the entrance to what I referred to as "My Secret Hiding Place." I smiled to myself as I looked around and thought of Grandma. She was the one who showed me this place. She had found a better way in on the other side of the house, but she nailed it up so Mama wouldn't find out. She then loosened the board that had become the entrance to my own little paradise.

I lay down on the old blanket Grandma had given me and quietly sobbed. I opened my hand to find the bread crumbled in a ball, but that was all right with me—it was food, and I was hungry.

I could hear them arguing above me. I covered my ears to block them out and thought of the day Grandma first showed me this place. Mama had gone into town that day. While she was gone, we made the most of what little time we had. Grandma spread this blanket on the ground, here in my secret place, and sat down on it. I sat down next to her, and she pulled me close, smiled tenderly, and said, "Close your eyes, my little Angel. I have a surprise for you."

I closed my eyes. I was so excited I could hardly sit still.

"Okay, you can look now."

I opened my eyes to find the most delicious-looking bologna sandwich sitting on a plate right in front of me. "Here, child." She handed me a glass of lemonade. I know a bologna sandwich and lemonade may not sound like much, but to someone who hasn't eaten for two days, it's a delicacy.

CHAPTER 8

THE HOSPITAL

A couple of hours later, sirens screamed up the road. Lights flashed as an ambulance pulled into our driveway.

Mama met them on the porch and led them into the house. They went into Grandma's room and tried to wake her up.

Mama told them Grandma had been sick for several days and refused to go to the doctor, no matter how hard she tried to get her to go. I wanted to run in there, shouting she was lying and tell them the truth about everything, but I feared what she would do to me, so I sat quietly in my secret place.

Curiosity and fear got the better of me, so I crawled until I came to the loose board and slid it over and carefully slipped out. I stayed close to the side of the house and made my way to the back, and then sneaked in the back door. They were in

Grandma's room, strapping her to a gurney. Mama had her by the hand with her back to me. I ran to my room.

I watched from my window as two paramedics carried Grandma down the steps on a gurney. They placed her in the ambulance, and then closed the double doors. Mama said she would meet them at the hospital; she ran back into the house to grab her purse and car keys.

I jumped back onto my bed when I heard her unlocking my door. I could see from the expression on her face she was worried.

"Stay here, Angela. I have to go to the hospital to be with your grandma. She is very sick, and they may have to keep her."

I had never seen Mama so worried about anyone or anything. I couldn't help but wonder if she was afraid for Grandma or herself. She stared at the floor for a moment. "If anyone comes, don't make a sound, and don't answer the door." She stood looking at me for a moment. She stooped down in front of me, looked me in the eyes and hugged me. "I'm sorry for the way I have treated you both. I love you, and I want to make things right," she said sadly.

I wasn't sure how to respond. She had apologized so many times. I wanted to believe her, but at the moment I just wanted her to leave me alone.

I looked down to see that my hands and clothes were dirty. I had to think of something quick, so I ran to the window and looked out. "They're leaving."

"I have to go." Mama backed out of the room and pulled the door shut. "Remember what I said," she yelled over her shoulder as she ran out the front door.

I watched as she backed the car, then started down the long dirt driveway, leaving a trail of dust behind her as she pulled onto the old dirt road, driving faster than usual trying to catch up with the ambulance. I waited until she was out of sight before walking over and twisting the doorknob. Just as I thought, she had forgotten to lock it.

The first thing I did was run into the kitchen, open the fridge, and grab a couple of slices of leftover bacon. *Oh, no. Mama probably knows how many pieces of bacon were left.* I put it back and looked through the cabinet. I found an open box of pre-sweetened cereal. After pouring some into a bowl and adding milk, I decided to take it outside and sit on the porch swing to eat it. I figured that way I could hear if Mama came back up the road—or anyone else, for that matter.

I had forgotten how good cereal and cold milk tasted as I sat there alone, enjoying every last bite. I went back to the kitchen, washed, dried, and put away the bowl and spoon. Next, I got two sandwich bags and filled one with cereal and the other with cookies. I knew not to get the ones out of the cookie jar—Mama always counted those. I remembered seeing an open package in the back of the cabinet when I got out the box of cereal. I figured it was safer to get some of those. Seven sounded like a good number, especially since that's how old I was. I tried to justify taking the cookies, since Mama didn't get me anything for my birthday last year. No cake, no ice cream, nothing. Unbeknownst to Mama, Grandma gave me a cupcake with a candle in it and a new coloring book and crayons.

I made sure to put everything back where I found it, hoping and praying that Mama wouldn't notice anything missing.

I checked one last time to make sure there were no crumbs or drops of milk anywhere before taking my snacks to my room and then hiding them under my bed.

I went to Grandmas' room and stood for a moment as sweet memories of her flooded in. "I miss you already," I whispered, brushing away a tear with the back of my hand. I could hear Mama's hateful words ringing in my head—*Nobody likes a crybaby, Angela.*

I'm not going to cry, I thought as I stood there looking around the room.

I loved the way Grandma's room always felt warm and welcoming. The walls were white, trimmed in pale yellow; the curtains were covered with a variety of colored flowers on a light yellow background. Hanging on one side of the window was the framed picture I'd colored for her. On the opposite side was a picture of me that Grandma had taken with her digital camera. She enlarged it on the computer and then printed it off.

She loved this room, and just like Mama, she kept everything spotless. She once told me her room reminded her of a warm spring morning. She loved spring and the outdoors, and her room reflected that. Her bed, which was always neatly made, stood unmade and empty in the center of the bedroom. A huge picture of Jesus hung above the bed, and a well-worn Bible lay on the nightstand next to the bed, along with a small touch lamp, an alarm clock, and an old wedding picture of Grandma and Grandpa.

I only knew him through stories Grandma shared with me. He died long before I was born. At the foot of the bed against the wall stood a dresser and mirror, and a flat-screen TV hung on the wall next to it. The closet was on the far end of the room. The thing I loved most of all was Grandma's bedspread. It was soft white and yellow chenille, with a basket of pink and blue flowers in the center of it. The best memory I had in this room was the day Grandma gave me my new birthday dress.

CHAPTER 9

PRAYERS FOR GRANDMA

I lay down on Grandma's bed and whispered a prayer for her. I had no idea what was going on. I wondered when or if she would come back home. Fear hit like a ton of bricks. What is Mama going to do if Grandma has to stay in the hospital? For that matter, what am I going to do? What will happen if she's not here to protect me? What if she dies? I'll never see her again, and I didn't even get to say goodbye. A tear rolled down my cheek. I tried to ignore all the thoughts that kept popping in my head, but no matter how much I tried not to think about it, the question remained. *What is going to happen?*

Even though Mama was sometimes hateful with Grandma or acted like she didn't care, I couldn't help but wonder if she was just pretending. After having one of her tantrums, it seemed to bother her if Grandma was disappointed or upset with her.

If anyone knows how that feels, it would be me. I try to please Mama, and I want so much for her to love me, but nothing I do is ever good enough in her eyes. Maybe she's right—I am unlovable. I quickly erased the thought from my mind. I knew I was loved, perhaps not by Mama, but at least by my grandma. She always made it a point to remind me how much she and God loved me. Even though I was grateful to have Grandma in my life, I needed and wanted the love that only a mother can give.

Kneeling down by the bed, I said a prayer not only for Grandma, but also for Mama.

After I finished praying, I stood and looked around the room, trying to decide what to do next. I started to straighten the bed, but quickly decided against it for fear Mama would know I'd been out of my room. You'd think she'd appreciate the help. But then again, this was my mother, and with her crazy mood swings, I wasn't taking any chances. I looked out the window when the dogs began to bark, but saw nothing. I walked into the kitchen and looked out the back door window and breathed a sigh of relief when I saw a cat race across the yard and disappear into the woods. I felt sorry for those dogs. If anyone could relate to what they were going through, it would be me. They were kept locked in a pen and abused the same as I was locked in my room, sometimes for days. For some reason, Mama wanted me to be afraid of them. She said they were mean and I should stay away from them, but Grandma and I not only visited but also fed them every chance we got. Grandma said it was a good idea to let them get used to us. That way, if they ever got out, they wouldn't harm us. I genuinely don't think any of them had a mean bone in their bodies.

I walked over to the counter and grabbed the bucket of scraps. I gripped the handle with both hands while holding it in front of me. It was heavier than I expected. I wobbled from side to side as I made my way out to the dog pen. They began barking again and climbing over each other, trying to be the first to get fed. I grabbed scraps of food by the handful—eggs, toast, and strips of bacon that was meant to be my breakfast, among a few other leftovers Mama threw in when she cleaned out the fridge this morning. I stuck my fingers through the fence and let the dogs lick them clean before taking the rest of the leftovers back to the kitchen and placing them on the counter where I found them. I went to the bathroom to wash my hands, making sure I dried the sink with a towel and threw it in the hamper before leaving the room.

I wandered around the house bored and alone. I went to the living room, turned on the television, and watched a few cartoons. I worried that I wouldn't hear if Mama returned, so I turned it off and then ran to the front door and listened. It was eerily quiet out. I turned and looked the living room over, making sure nothing was out of place. The house had hardwood flooring throughout, which Mama kept at a polished shine. The couch sat in the middle of the floor with an end table at each end. A massive stone fireplace stood against the wall in front of it. A chair was positioned at one end of the room, and the television on the other. A large oval rug lay on the floor underneath the coffee table. The kitchen was at the back on the left. There was a staircase at the end of the wall on the right, facing the front door. It led to Mama's room. I was forbidden to go up there, so I had never seen that part of the house. My room was off from the living room in the front of the house next to Grandma's. I often wondered what the upstairs looked like. I even contemplated going up and checking it out, but decided against it, as fear overrode curiosity.

I walked out on the front porch, sat on the bottom step, and waited for Old Man Sims' dogs to sound the alarm of Mama and Grandma's return. After sitting for what seemed like hours with no sign of anyone coming, and growing more bored than before, I made up my mind that I would go to my room and color Grandma another picture—and also surprise Mama with one.

After checking the kitchen one last time, making sure I'd left everything the way it was, I went back to my room and closed the door. I was unsure of what to do.

Questions raced through my mind. *Did Mama forget to lock my door? Was this a test to see if I would leave my room? Or did she have a heart and leave it unlocked on purpose, so I could get something to eat?*

"Nah," I thought, shaking my head. I knew better than that. But it was a nice thought.

My mind wandered back to the book, picture and the voices I'd heard. With everything that had been going on around here, it had slipped my mind, but now as I sat alone, fear began to set in. I jumped when the house creaked above my head. I could feel my heart beating in my chest. Deciding I would feel safer outside, I eased myself off the bed, my feet feeling as though they were weighed down by bricks, becoming heavier with each step.

I heard a car pull up the driveway. I walked over and looked out the window. It was Mama. She had her hands full of shopping bags. My heart sank when I saw she was alone.

She hurried up the stairs and into the house.

I made it back to my bed just as she burst into my room.

I jumped and nearly fell off the bed.

"Angela, put these on. Quick." She handed me a new pair of blue jeans and a pink t-shirt with yellow and orange flowers and dark pink, blue and purple butterflies hovering diagonally from the bottom right corner to the left shoulder.

"Wow!" I exclaimed. "That's the prettiest shirt I've ever seen. Thanks, I love it."

"I thought you might," she said.

"Don't tell Grandma, but I think it's prettier than my dress," I whispered, even though I knew Grandma wasn't there and I didn't honestly think that. I just wanted to please Mama.

She smiled and hugged me. I don't remember her ever doing that for no reason.

She held a box out in front of her, which I happily received and sat on the floor to open.

"Go ahead and open it," she said, smiling.

I lifted the lid to reveal a pack of new socks. Underneath the socks were a new pair of purple and pink tennis shoes, which also had a butterfly on the side of each one.

"They are beautiful, and they match my shirt. Thank you, Mama."

"I'm glad you like them. I also have some new panties for you," Mama added. "I stopped at the store and bought all this stuff just for you. I want you to look nice when I take you to the hospital with me to visit Grandma—which we're getting ready to do right now. So, I need you to get dressed as fast as you can." She turned and left the room while I got ready.

I didn't know what had come over Mama that was causing her to be so sweet, nor did I care. I was happy to see this side of her, and I was going to enjoy every minute of it while it lasted. I quickly got dressed, put on my socks and shoes, and sat for a moment staring at the floor.

Mama came in and asked what was wrong. I was afraid to tell her I didn't know how to tie my shoes. She must have sensed what the problem was, because she bent over without saying a word and tied them.

"There now, run and get in the car, and I'll be there in a moment. I just have to grab a few things your grandma may need."

I climbed into the backseat of the car and waited. I was both excited and nervous at the same time.

After a few minutes, Mama came out and strapped me in, since I had no idea how to use a seatbelt in the first place. The car, like the house, was spotless and smelled terrific. I asked Mama what scent it smelled like. She said it was something called Hawaiian paradise. I told her I would love for my bedroom to smell like that. She said she'd buy an air freshener just like it, for my room, as soon as we got back from visiting Grandma.

This side of her was kind of odd and different. I liked her this way, but I also knew I had to keep my guard up.

The ride was tranquil as we worked our way down the winding road leading off the mountain. I got a good look at all the dogs when we passed Old Man Sims' place. Some were in pens and others tied to dog houses. All were barking at once. Two little tan-colored dogs ran to the edge of the porch and joined in. Mama called them loud-mouth Chihuahuas. I thought they were cute. Three more ran out of nowhere and chased us down the road. I laughed as one ran alongside the car, barking at me as I looked out the window.

"Do you know what he's saying, Angela?" Mom asked.

"No," I said shaking my head.

"He's saying, 'Hey, little girl,'" she said in a deep voice, "'Let me in. I want to go to town with you.'"

I had never laughed so hard in my life. We were both laughing and wiping tears from of our eyes.

"You're funny," I said.

"Yeah, your mama's a real comedian, huh, baby?" She laughed.

After that, we rode in silence the rest of the way down the mountain. The only noise was the hum of the engine and the radio softly playing in the background.

CHAPTER 10

THE CONFRONTATION

We pulled into the hospital parking lot to find the place packed with cars. Mama told me to keep an eye out for an empty parking space. After circling the lot several times, she noticed someone pulling out of a space. She turned on her signal light and impatiently waited for them to leave, grumbling under her breath all the while. But we finally parked.

We rushed into the emergency room and approached the registration desk. A lady who looked to be about the same age as Mama was talking to the receptionist.

Mama stepped forward. "Excuse me, my mother was—"

The receptionist glanced up. "Ma'am, I'm helping this lady. Step in line, and I'll be with you in a moment."

Mama stepped back in line and paced back and forth, growing more impatient with every step. The line of people waiting grew longer by the minute.

After several minutes passed, Mama stepped forward and was once again cut short and told to wait in line.

"Remember when we were in school and we both had a crush on Bobby Spencer?" the woman in front of her asked the receptionist.

"Oh! My goodness, I forgot about that." The receptionist giggled.

Several people in line muttered their annoyance with the situation. "I wish they would hurry up," whispered one man to his wife.

A young woman stepped to the front of the line. "I'm just here to visit a friend, and all I need is the room number."

"Get back in line, please," the receptionist said with an icy stare.

By this time, Mama had had enough. She grabbed the woman in front of her by the arm, moving her out of the way.

"What do you think you're doing?" the woman said, shocked.

"Your best bet is to walk away." Mama pointed her finger in the lady's face.

The woman could see from the look in Mama's eyes that she was not joking. "I'll call you later, Mary," the lady yelled to the receptionist, then quickly walked away.

Mama turned her attention to the receptionist.

She had scooted her chair back out of reach. "Calm down, ma'am. Don't make me call security."

"Go ahead and reach for that phone," Mama said in a low, angry voice. "I'll break every bone in your hand before they get here. Do you understand? *Mary?*" Mama said in a threatening tone, all the while staring at her with those piercing evil eyes I knew all too well.

"Yes, ma'am," she said, her eyes wide with horror.

"Now, I am going to say this once and only once, so listen carefully." Mama scoffed. "An ambulance brought my mother here about three hours ago. I had already registered her when I was here earlier. I need you to tell me if they have admitted her yet, and, if so, what is the number of her room? If not, then point me in the direction they have taken her. Is that clear, Mary?"

"Yes," Mary said, a stiff smile on her lips.

"After that," continued Mama, leaning over the desk, "I suggest you keep your mouth shut and do your job. These people behind me have been patiently waiting in line, listening to you gossiping and reminiscing long enough. If you can't do your job, I'm sure they can find someone who can. Do I need to speak to someone in charge? Or maybe I should talk to the chief of staff, whom just so happens to be a family friend?" she lied.

The whole room exploded with applause.

"No, that won't be necessary," the receptionist replied, her voice quivering. She pointed toward the right. "Go through the double doors, and a nurse will take you to your mother."

"Now, that's more like it." Mama smirked, taking me by the hand and leading me through the double doors, which led to another large waiting room. The entire left wall was nothing but windows. We walked past a small hallway leading to the restrooms. Next was a room full of different kinds of vending machines. I had never seen anything like it.

"Look, Mama." I pointed, amazed at all the different candy and chips and soda.

"I see it." Mama gave me a little tug.

We approached another desk, only this time the receptionist was much more helpful.

"Hello, Margret, how are you today?" the receptionist asked politely.

"Hello, Beth. I'm fine. An ambulance brought my mother in a little while ago."

"Oh, no!" Beth said. "I hope she wasn't involved in an accident."

"No, it wasn't an accident, but she is very sick. I'm trying to find out where they took her."

"I can help you with that," Beth said. "Just give me one second, and I'll see if she's here. What's your mother's name?"

"Baker, Virginia Baker."

"I just call her *Grandma*," I said with a grin.

"What a pretty little girl you are, and who might you be?" Beth asked.

"I'm Angela, but my grandma calls me Angel," I whispered with my hands cupped around each side of my mouth.

"I'd have to agree with your grandma. You're pretty enough to be an angel," Beth said.

"Sorry I had to cancel our visit," Mama said. "But as you can see, I have my hands full with my mother being sick."

"Now, don't you worry about that. I understand completely. We can always plan a play date for the girls another time. You just make sure to take care of this lovely little lady and your mama first." Beth stood and called over a nurse. "Do you know anything about the Baker woman who was brought in by ambulance?"

"You mean the one in the accident?" the nurse asked.

"No, that was Barker. The one I am inquiring about is Ms. Baker. She was brought in not long ago with breathing problems."

"Oh! Yes, that one." The nurse looked at Mama. "Are you a relative?"

"Yes, I'm her daughter," Mama answered.

"Okay, then, come with me." The nurse led the way. "She was just admitted to ICU. Your mother is a very sick lady. The doctor will explain everything to you as soon as we get all the test results back."

She led us through a door, down a long hallway, and through a set of double doors. She pushed a big silver button on the wall to the left.

"If you don't mind waiting in there," she said, pointing to a waiting room to the right of us, "I will check and see if she's ready to receive visitors."

We no sooner sat down when the nurse returned and told us we could go in.

"Can I go?" I asked

"I don't see why not," the nurse replied. "We think it's good for patients to see their children and grandchildren—as long as you are very quiet. Besides, she has been asking for you."

She led us through the double doors and to a room at the end, straight across from the nurses' desk. Windows surrounded the place.

I slowly walked up to her bedside and touched her hand. "Grandma," I whispered.

"Shhh, she's asleep." Mama picked me up so I could get a better look.

Grandma was hooked up to tubes and machines; I had never seen anything like it. I asked a lot of questions, and the nurse patiently answered every one. I was surprised Mama didn't stop me, but I learned that the tube in Grandma's arm was an IV and the one in her nose was to help her breathe. And it was hooked to a machine that provided her with oxygen.

A tall, medium-built man entered the room dressed in a pair of dress pants and a button-up shirt and tie, all covered with a long white jacket. His jet black hair showed specks of gray throughout, making him look very distinguished. He was a nice-looking man.

"Hello, I'm Dr. Ross." He extended his hand.

Mama shook his hand and smiled, but not just any smile. There was a twinkle in her eye. "Hello, I'm Margret." She twisted a strand of hair around her finger, something I had never seen her do before.

I could tell right away that Mama was quite taken with him. She straightened her shirt, ran her fingers through her hair, and watched transfixed, her mouth agape as he spoke to the nurse.

He woke Grandma to ask her a few questions while placing the stethoscope on her chest. "Take a deep breath," he said.

Grandma obeyed.

"Exhale." His expression seemed puzzled. "Okay, and once more."

Grandma began coughing and could hardly catch her breath.

He stood. "Okay, get some rest, and I will be back to check on you later." He patted her hand and smiled.

"May I speak to you alone?" he asked Mama.

She followed him out and down the hallway. With the windows everywhere, I could still see them, although I couldn't hear anything. Mama shook her head and talked with her hands. She usually did that when she was either excited or angry. I could tell right away it was the latter.

Grandma began to stir a little.

Reaching up and taking her hand, I whispered. "I love you, Grandma."

She awoke and smiled faintly. "I love you, too, my little Angel. I was hoping you would come."

"How are you feeling?" I choked back tears.

"I'm feeling a little better than I was this morning. It must be all the meds."

"I'm glad you're feeling better. I miss you so much and can't wait for you to come home."

"I can't wait to get home and finish making all your beautiful dresses for you. I want to see you in every one of them."

I told her all about how Mama came home with new clothes for me and how sweet she was being.

Grandma complimented me on my new outfit and shoes. "They look very nice. I'm glad Mama is finally coming around, but be careful and don't do anything to upset her."

We both knew the slightest things would set Mama off, and I was always the one who paid—and paid dearly.

A look of concern replaced Grandma's smile. She began to cough, which made it more difficult for her to breathe. I wanted to run and get the nurse, but she wouldn't let go of my hand. The coughing subsided, and she was finally able to speak. "Angela, I need you to do something for me."

"Okay, Grandma, I will. What is it?"

"I need you to pray for me. I'm going to be okay. I just need you to pray and agree with me. With both of us praying for the same thing, God is sure to hear and answer us."

I squeezed her hand. "Don't worry, Grandma, I have been praying for you, and I have faith that God is going to take care of you."

Mama entered the room, brushing a tear from her eye. It was the first time I'd seen Mama show any emotion other than anger. I wanted to know what the doctor told her, but decided it would be better not to ask questions. I couldn't help but wonder what she was up to. She was still acting nice—maybe even a little too nice. I knew better than anyone that was not a good sign. I wasn't quite sure what had gotten into her lately, nor did I care. I was going to enjoy it while it lasted.

CHAPTER 11

NEW FRIENDS

As our visit came to a close, we said a tearful goodbye and left the hospital. We pulled onto the highway and started for home. Everything was quiet except for the hum of the motor and the sound of tires hitting the pavement.

"Angela, are you hungry?" Mama asked.

Oh, no! Is this her way of asking if I got into the cookies? My body was becoming tense, and I nervously fumbled with the seatbelt.

"Yes, ma'am," I whispered. *Oh lord! She knows about the cereal and cookies. I just know she does.* My mind raced as I tried to think of something to say. Maybe I should tell her the truth and get it over with. I knew I was in trouble, but telling her would at least be better than waiting and wondering. Sometimes I think the waiting and knowing what was coming was worse than the beating itself. With all the courage I could muster, I decided to confess.

"Mama," I whispered.

No answer. She was talking to herself. *Uh-oh. That's never a good sign.*

"Mama," I said a little louder.

"Huh, did you say something?" she asked, looking straight ahead.

"Are you mad at me?" I asked, my voice quivering.

"Now why would I be mad at you?" she asked sweetly. "You were a very good girl today. All the nurses were bragging on you. I am very proud of you, and that's why I'm going to take you out to eat and get you whatever you want."

I sat there, unsure of how to respond. I had already been through the whole breakfast ordeal with Mama that morning, so I was afraid to show any reaction for fear it was another lie.

"Angela, did you hear what I said?" she asked between glances at me and the road.

I sat wringing my hands in my lap and slowly nodded.

"Well, then, at least show a little excitement. I'm trying to do something nice for you today."

"Do I get to eat with you this time, Mama?"

"Yes, you do, and not only that, we are eating out, so where do you want to go?"

"Oh, goody!" I yelled, clapping my hands and bouncing on the seat. "You choose." I was so thrilled I could hardly sit still, and this time Mama didn't yell at me for it.

"Hmmm, now let's see," she said softly to herself. "Where should we go? I know, how about pizza for lunch? How does that sound?"

"What is pizza?" I asked, thinking what a funny word that was.

Mama jerked her head around and looked at me for a second before saying, "Oh my goodness, I forgot how much you haven't done or tried. You'll see. So pizza it is, and you are going to love it."

We pulled into the parking lot in front of an enormous red building. It had lots of windows with pictures of food plastered all over them. There was a big red and white sign that said PIZZA PLACE. I was giddy with excitement as I skipped along holding Mama's hand. The first thing I noticed as we entered were all the kids, most of which were my age. They were laughing and playing in a huge thing made of tubes and a slide. I hadn't been off the mountain since I was a baby. Therefore, everything was exciting and new for me. I couldn't help but wonder if the whole world was like this, full of kids to play with, the smell of good food, and people everywhere. I loved it—all of it. I didn't want to go back home.

The pizza was fantastic. I had never tasted anything like it, and I could hardly sit still to eat it. Mama laughed and asked if I liked it. I nodded and finished eating. I asked if I could play with the other kids in the tubes and was told to go ahead. I had the best day of my life.

That's the day I met Carol. She was the little girl who was supposed to have come for a playdate. Her mother was Mama's friend, the receptionist at the hospital. They met up with us at the Pizza Place. Carol and I got along from the moment we met. We played and laughed until our sides hurt. Mama even enjoyed herself. It was nice to see her smiling and laughing aloud. And for the first time, I noticed that she had lost a lot of weight. Maybe Grandma was right. God does answer prayers.

After leaving the Pizza Place, we went to the park. I was amazed that there were kids there, and also at all the stuff to play on. We laughed as we got on the swings. I had never seen one before, so I had no idea how to work it; but after some coaching and encouragement from Carol, I managed just fine. I got a little nervous the higher I swung until Carol showed me how to slow it down. It was smooth sailing after that. I loved the freedom I felt soaring through the air, the wind in my hair, soaring high above the ground

"Look at me, I'm a bird," I yelled.

"So am I," Carol said laughing.

We spent the better part of the day right there in the park. Swinging, playing on the slides, and riding the merry-go-round. We were having a great time—that was, until we made our way over to the sandbox. All the other kids had deserted it, except for one little dark-haired boy who was playing by himself. He wore a red and white striped shirt and blue jeans, and he held a yellow plastic shovel in his hand. We decided to join him.

"Hello, what's your name?" I asked. I could tell this wasn't going to go well when he looked up at us and growled. I stepped back, unsure of what was wrong with him or what he might do.

But not Carol. She placed her hands on her hips and never took her eyes off him. "Did you just growl like a dog?"

"I'm not a dog. I am a wolf," he replied. "This is my sandbox, and you can't play in it."

"You wanna bet?" Carol stepped into the sandbox.

"Hey! You can't play in here," he yelled.

"You don't own it," Carol retorted, placing her hands on her hips once again and leaning forward with her face in his; she was now almost nose to nose with him.

"Yes, I do. Now get out, you can't play!"

"Yes, we can! Come on, Angela," she said, motioning for me to get in. I stepped in by her, and that's when it all went from bad to worse. He pushed her down, then picked up a shovel full of sand and dumped it on top of her head, not only getting it in her eyes but also her mouth. Carol, who was so upset, began to cry. I don't know what came over me. I was so mad I could feel anger boiling in the pit of my stomach. Before I realized it, I yelled, "You can't do that to my best friend!" Balling my hand into a fist, I punched him square on the nose.

He stumbled out of the sandbox and lay on the ground, writhing and crying like he was dying. I turned in time to see his mother running toward us. She grabbed me by the arm and started yelling profanities at me and something about me being a brat and how I should be kept home away from other kids.

For once in my life, I was actually glad when I thought of Mama. With all her diabolical, scheming tactics, she would know how to deal with this situation. Looking around through tear-filled eyes, I tried to pinpoint her location. Fortunately for me, she had seen the whole thing.

She grabbed the boy's mother by the hair, yanking hard. "You have two seconds to turn my daughter lose, or I will snap your neck like twig," she said between gritted teeth.

The woman immediately released her grip. I ran to check on Carol. She had already spit out the sand that was in her mouth and was still rubbing her eyes. Beth was trying to calm her while brushing sand out of her hair.

"I'm sorry he was mean to you, Carol," I said sadly.

"I don't like him, and I'm glad you punched him in the nose," she replied between sobs.

Beth, smiling, whispered a thank you and winked at me. "Even though I don't condone fighting," she said, "I'm so glad you girls stood up to that bully."

I don't know what Mama was saying to the boy and his mother, but whatever it was, it couldn't have been good because the lady grabbed her son and hurried out of the park.

CHAPTER 12

VISITING GRANDMA

Carol and I were laughing by the time Mama walked over to where we were sitting on the grass.

But when I looked up at Mama, fear cut through me like a knife. "I'm sorry, Mama. Am I in trouble?" I asked nervously.

"No, you're not in trouble," she answered calmly. "You did what you had to do, and I am proud of you for it. Beth and I saw the whole thing. I don't think he will mess with you girls anymore."

Wow! That made the second time today that Mama said she was proud of me. I didn't know what happened that caused such a drastic change in her, but I liked it.

We sat laughing and talking about what happened. Carol was completely calm by now, and most of the sand was brushed out of her hair . "Now that that's over, why don't we take the girls out for an ice cream cone before heading home?" Beth asked.

"Yay! Ice cream! I want chocolate," yelled Carol.

"Me too," I said with a grin.

We stopped at the local dairy bar, and then waited patiently at one of the picnic tables while Mama and Beth placed the order.

It was the most delicious ice cream I'd ever had. I'm not sure if it was the ice cream or the fact that for once in my life I was happy. Whatever the case, I knew I would never forget this day. I had such a wonderful time I hated to see it end.

Mama and Beth set up another play date for us the following week. I was so excited I could hardly wait.

We decided to visit Grandma once more before returning home. She was looking a lot better this evening. She was sitting up and eating dinner when we got there.

"Boy, Grandma, you're a slow eater," I said.

She thought for a moment, and then laughed and said, "No, baby, this is my dinner. They brought lunch when you were here earlier."

Even Mama laughed aloud.

"It's so good to hear you laugh again, Margret."

"Well, Mother, I have something to be happy about."

"And what would that be? You haven't met a man, have you?"

"Lord, no, Mother. But I did have an incredible day with a new friend. And no! She is not a man. She works here at the hospital. Her name is Beth, and she has a little girl the same age as Angela. And for the first time in a long time, I am happy."

"By the way," Mama continued, moving closer to Grandma. "You really scared me this morning. And it got me to thinking. I don't know what I would do if I ever lost either of you. So, I am making some much-needed changes in my life. Things are going to be different when you come home, you'll see. I have already started a weight loss plan, and I'm going to stick with it this time."

Grandma smiled, tears pooling in her eyes. "I am so happy to hear that, Margret. All I ever wanted is for you and Angela to be happy. It's what I have been praying for, and as for as the weight loss, I have faith that you can do anything you set your mind to."

"Thank you." Mama's eyes teared up as she leaned over, giving Grandma a gentle hug. She quickly rose up, rubbed the tears from her eyes, and straightened her clothes. "Okay, enough about me," she said, and looked at me. "Angela, would you like to tell Grandma what we did today?"

"Yes, ma'am," I said excitedly. I told Grandma about my day and my new friend. I must have been talking too fast, because she had to keep reminding me to slow down. I'll never forget the wide-eyed expression on Grandma's face when I got to the part where I punched the boy in the nose. Mama explained the whole situation to her. Grandma lectured me on fighting, but also added that she was very proud of me for standing my ground where that bully was concerned and for coming to the aid of my friend.

We spent the next couple hours visiting with Grandma, laughing and talking. It was nice; I wondered if I was dreaming, and prayed if I were, then I wouldn't wake up. I wasn't ready to go back to the way things were.

"I'll be right back," Mama said.

We watched her leave, then Grandma pulled me close to her. "You know your Mama has gone through stages before when she would be sweet for a short period. But then something makes her mad and she takes it out on you. I'm worried about leaving you alone with her."

"I'll be okay," I said. "I know how to watch her."

Grandma held me tight. "You just be very careful, okay?"

"Yes, ma'am."

A tap on the door frame caught my attention. I turned to see a man standing in the doorway, smiling. He was dressed in a black suit and carried a bible and a clipboard.

"Well, well, Virginia Baker, is that you?" The man was now standing at the foot of the bed.

The confused look left Grandma's face and was replaced with a huge smile. "Well, as I live and breathe, John Moore, I haven't seen you since High School. How have you been?

"I'm fine, and it's Pastor Moore now." He smiled.

"That's wonderful. I am happy to hear that." Grandma began to cough. "So what brings you to the hospital?" she asked after the coughing subsided.

"I come here a few times per week and pray for the sick," he answered. "I could pray for you, if you like."

"I would love that. I could use all the prayer I can get." Grandma wiped her mouth on a tissue..

"And who might this pretty young lady be?" Pastor Moore nodded toward me.

"My name is Angela, but you can call me Angel, if you like. That's what Grandma calls me." I grinned proudly.

"Then Angel it is." He smiled. "Would you like to draw a picture for your grandma to hang on her wall?" He handed me his clipboard. On it was a plain sheet of paper and a pencil.

I gladly took it and sat down on a chair next to the window and drew the first thing that popped in my head. When finished, I handed it to Grandma and smiled proudly, waiting for her response.

"Oh my lord! Angel, where in the world did you see something like this?" She handed the drawing to Pastor Moore.

"Do you not like it?" I asked, puzzled by their expressions.

"Angel, honey, where did you see this symbol?" Pastor Moore asked.

"I saw it in the scary story book Mama reads," I responded. "Only I don't like the picture of the devil with the glowing red eyes on the inside. It scares me," I whispered.

"Angel, I need you to promise that you will never draw this symbol again. It is an upside down pentagram, and it represents evil," Pastor Moore said.

"What about the star on the front cover with the circle around it? Is it bad?" I asked.

I could see the concern in Grandma's eyes. "It's all bad. Promise you will never touch that book or draw anything you saw in it again."

"I promise," I answered sadly. "Are you upset with me?"

"No, baby, I'm not, but I am upset with your Mama. She knows better than to play around with witchcraft. Not only is it evil, but it is also dangerous." She asked Pastor Moore to get rid of the drawing. He said a prayer and tore it into shreds.

"Virginia, may I have prayer with the two of you before I leave?" Pastor Moore asked.

"Please do, and would you please keep my daughter Margret in your prayers as well?"

"Yes, of course," the pastor answered.

We joined hands with the pastor and he said a prayer of protection for all of us. I must say I felt safer afterwards, knowing God would send angels to watch over me while Grandma was recovering in the hospital.

"We must keep this between us until I am well enough to leave," Grandma said, looking at the pastor, who nodded in agreement. Her gaze then settled on me. "Angel, I need for you to act as normal as possible around your mama. I don't want her to know about this conversation. Can you do that for me?"

"Yes, ma'am," I answered.

Pastor Moore handed Grandma his card. "Here is my number, and also the number to my church, should you need anything. Call anytime day or night." He paused at the door. "God be with you."

Soon, Mama walked back into the room. She carried two steaming cups. "Would you like a cup of hot cocoa?" she asked me.

I don't know who was more surprised, Grandma or me.

I sat on a chair the nurse placed in the corner when we arrived and slowly sipped my cocoa. It was delicious. I hardly ever got chocolate, so I savored every sip until it was all gone.

Mama sat on the bed next to Grandma; they were talking and laughing. I had no idea what they were saying, nor did I care. I was just happy seeing them laughing and getting along for a change. Come to think of it, I don't remember them ever sitting together and laughing or talking much, for that matter.

A woman's voice came over the intercom announcing that visiting hours were now over. We said our goodbyes and I promised to return tomorrow. I hugged Grandma, and she whispered in my ear, "Be on your best behavior and please be careful."

"I will, I promise," I whispered back.

She smiled and patted my hand. I looked back as I was walking out of the room. I thought I saw a tear slowly roll down her cheek.

I often wondered if it was a tear of happiness for the changes in Mama, sadness to see us go, or fear of what was to come.

CHAPTER 13

CHANGES

The ride home was calm and peaceful. I sat staring out the window, watching the trees turn into green blurs as we drove past. I thought of all the things we had done that day and how much things had changed since that morning. I said a silent prayer and thanked God for everything. If Mama meant what she said, life would be much better for all of us.

I drifted off into peaceful slumber. And, for the first time, I slept comfortably without worry or fear. I awoke upon hearing the car door slam and Mama softly calling my name. She opened the door, leaned in, scooped me up into her arms and carried me into the house, and then gently lay me on my bed. I was so tired, and for the first time for as long as I could remember, I wasn't going to bed hungry.

I awoke the next morning, wondering, hoping and praying it wasn't all a dream. I slowly got out of bed and walked into the living room. The house was still and quiet. I wondered if Mama had left to see Grandma without me. I crossed my fingers, and for the first time, I hoped I wasn't home alone. I entered the kitchen and found it empty. I looked through the backdoor window and saw her feeding the dogs. She was yelling at them to stay down, as usual. My first instinct was to do what I always did, and that was to take a chance and raid the cookie jar, hoping she hadn't counted them, but decided otherwise.

I reluctantly returned to Grandma's room, praying to find her there. A wave of sadness rushed over me to find her room empty. I ran my hand over her bedspread, so soft and inviting. I lay my head on it and took in the freshly laundered smell.

I heard a noise behind me and jumped. I turned to see Mama in the doorway. I immediately began to shake. I knew better than to be in Grandma's room when she wasn't home. I stood wringing my hands, trying hard to think of an explanation. My mind blank, so I sat down and began to cry, awaiting my punishment.

Mama quickly came to my side and sat on the floor next to me. "It's okay, baby; I miss her too."

What? I thought, *She thinks I'm crying because I miss Grandma.* I wasn't quite sure how to react to her and the affection she was trying to show, so my mood was guarded. Upon realizing I wasn't in trouble, I stopped trembling and calmed down enough to speak. "When is Grandma coming home? I miss her and want her here with us."

"That is sweet," she said. "I think your grandma would like that too, but you know she is very sick, and she needs a few weeks of bed rest and medication before she can come home."

"How long will that take?" I asked.

"Remember what your Grandma said?"

I thought for a moment. "Grandma said that when I get ready for bed each night, count that as one sleep, and by the time I get to fourteen, she will be home, if not before then."

"That's right. You have already had one sleep, so that leaves thirteen or less to go, but I'll tell you a little secret," she said soothingly. "The doctor said she might only be in there for a week—seven days. It all depends on how well the meds work. Now, how about some breakfast?"

I could hardly wait for Grandma to come home. Things just weren't the same without her. I decided to keep myself preoccupied with whatever I could to stay out of Mama's sight. I figured that way she wouldn't have an excuse to get angry with me. But then again, this was Mama I was talking about. She would get upset over the smallest things, depending on what kind of mood she was in. I was glad that whatever put her in such a good mood yesterday had carried over into today.

"Come to the kitchen with me, and I will show you how to make breakfast. Are you hungry?"

"Yes, ma'am, I am."

"Well, then how about some pancakes and syrup?"

"Yum, I love pancakes. I want to make some for Grandma when she comes home."

I sat at the kitchen table and waited for Mama to get things ready. She poured everything into a bowl and then handed me a spoon. I had a wonderful time learning how to cook, but the best part was eating and spending quality time with Mama. After breakfast, I helped clean the kitchen and wash the dishes. It was more fun than I thought it would be.

Afterwards, Mama called Beth and invited her to come up so Carol and I could have a playdate. I ran to my room and began planning what we could do for the day. Mama bought a bunch of new toys for Carol and me to play with. I thought she bought them because she wanted to change and wanted me to be happy, but I soon learned she was trying to impress Beth. She was pretending to be the best mother in the world, and I feared it was just a matter of time before that grew old and her true colors would come shining through. I couldn't think about such things right now. I needed to focus on one day at a time, especially today. The thought of my friend coming to see me brought a smile to my face. *My friend*—I loved the sound of that.

I sat on the porch swing awaiting their arrival. Mama was in the kitchen making lunch. I had no idea what she was making, but it smelled wonderful. In the meantime, she called Old Man Sims and asked if he wanted our dogs. If not, then they were going to the pound. He said he would come right away to retrieve them. I opened the front door and yelled to alert her of his arrival. She came out, and they headed around back to take a look at the dogs. A few minutes later, Old Man Sims returned to his truck. After several tries, he managed to get it started, and then drove around the house where he and Mama proceeded to load the dogs into the cages, he brought with him. He climbed back into his truck and was about to leave when she asked him to wait. She quickly ran into the house and returned several minutes later holding a covered dish.

"I hope you like homemade lasagna," she said with a smile. "It's to show my appreciation for taking the dogs off my hands."

A huge smile spread across Old Man Sims' face as he took it and gently placed it on the seat beside him. "It has been a long time since I've had a home-cooked meal, and lasagna was always my favorite." I'm not sure which excited him more—the dogs or the meal. "Thank you, ma'am," he said as he tipped his hat and then waved to me as he slowly drove off.

CHAPTER 14

THE BROKEN VASE

The day had started out beautifully, and I had a feeling it was going to get better, much better, now that Carol was coming to play. Old Man Sims' dogs alerted me to their coming. I ran into the house to let Mama know.

"Mama!" I yelled, running into the living room. Mama had been cleaning and had moved a table. I bumped into it, sending a vase flying through the air. It shattered into a thousand pieces. For a split second, I caught a glimpse of evil in Mama's eyes just as she drew back her fist to punch me.

"Beth is coming up the road!" I yelled.

She lowered her hand to her side, and with a forced smile, she said, "We will talk about this later."

"I'm sorry, Mama. I didn't mean to break the vase. I'll clean it up." I stooped down and picked up a shard of glass.

"No, I'll do it," she said, grabbing me by the arm and moving me out of the way. "You are so clumsy, Angela, and I don't need you getting cut and bleeding all over everything. Go out on the porch and let me know when you see them."

I turned and ran out onto the front porch just as Beth's car appeared down the road. I was so excited that I wanted to jump, scream, shout, or something, but I knew better. I had already upset Mama once today. I was not going to try her patience again. Maybe if I stayed out of sight for the rest of the day, maybe, just maybe, she would forget about the broken vase.

"They're coming!" I yelled. "I can see them just down the road."

"Okay," she said, standing in the doorway. "Angela, I want you to be on your best behavior. I am warning you, if you do one more stupid thing today, after they leave you will get the beating of your life. Do you understand?"

"Yes, ma'am. I'll be good. I promise."

Beth pulled into the driveway. The car had barely stopped when Carol opened the car door and jumped out. She was as excited as I was. She ran to me and gave me a big hug. I didn't know how to react; I had never had a friend before. We hugged each other as we jumped up and down, giggling.

"Well, I see a couple of girls are going to have a good time today," Beth laughed.

"Sure looks that way," Mama said, smiling.

Carol and I went to my room to play while Mama and Beth headed for the kitchen. I could hardly wait to show her all the new toys. I hadn't so much as touched them. I was saving them for this day with my best friend. Besides, Mama wouldn't let me play with them. She said she didn't want me to get them dirty before Beth and Carol had a chance to see them.

After several hours, Beth showed up at the bedroom door and announced that lunch was ready. We ran, giggling, to the kitchen, and found a place at the table. I took a bite of lasagna, and it set my taste buds to dancing. It was the best meal I'd ever had—except for the pizza we had yesterday.

"This is good, Mama. Do you think I can have lunch like this every day?" I knew from the expression on Mama's face that I had said something wrong.

Thank goodness Beth saved the day when she laughed and said, "Well, Margret, I think she just paid you a compliment. You should be very proud."

The look on Mama's face softened. She smiled, and then hugged me. I knew it was a fake gesture, and I also knew that I was in big trouble as soon as Beth and Carol were gone. I had an awful feeling in the pit of my stomach.

After lunch, Carol and I ran outside to play. We started chasing butterflies, but just as we would get close enough to catch one, it flew away. We played hide and seek, tag, and several other games she taught me. We worked up a sweat and decided to get a cold drink of water from the water hose. I turned it on, but nothing came out. Carol looked into the hose to see if it was clogged. It wasn't. We just couldn't figure out what the problem was. That is until I found a kink in the hose and straightened it out. Carol, who at that moment decided to look into the end of the hose ended up with a face full of water. I stood frozen, not sure what to expect. To my chagrin, she turned the hose on me and soaked me good.

We were laughing and enjoying ourselves. But when Mama and Beth caught us, I knew we were in for it. Beth marched up and grabbed the hose out of Carol's hand, not once cracking a smile. She then did something that caught us all off guard. Beth turned the hose on Mama, soaking her from head to toe.

Mama gasped, and the look on her face was priceless.

I stood with my mouth open, waiting for an angry outburst, but much to my surprise, she started laughing, and then she took the hose and sprayed water on all of us. Everyone fell to the ground, bursting into laughter. I must admit it was good seeing her laughing and playing. I liked her much better this way. But somewhere deep down inside I knew it wasn't going to last, and the thought of that scared me more than anything.

CHAPTER 15

ALONE WITH MAMA

Mama went inside to grab some towels while we sat on the front porch to dry off. She returned with not only towels, but also some cookies and milk for Carol and me. Maybe she really had changed, and things were going to be different.

"Angela, I'm talking to you," Carol said.

"What?" I asked

"I asked what your favorite kind of cookie is," she answered sounding a little annoyed at having to repeat the question.

"Oh, I don't know, I like them all," I answered. Then, looking over at Mama, I smiled and added, "But if you ask me, my Mama's cookies are better than any store-bought cookie. I would even say they are the best cookies in West Virginia."

I knew I'd said something right when a very proud smile spread across her face.

"I do believe that is the sweetest thing I have ever heard," Beth said. "You must be very proud to have such a sweet, loving little girl."

Yep, Mama was glowing with pride. And I was learning how to manipulate the situation by flattering her.

I also smiled with pride, not about Mama, but the fact that I finally understood what Grandma was trying to teach me all along. And that was that flattery will get you almost everywhere, and a kind word goes a long way.

We laughed and told jokes while we waited for our clothes to dry. We had a wonderful, fun-filled day. I closed my eyes, taking it all in. I was lost in thought when Beth announced it was time to leave. We'd had a full day, and everyone was tired.

Mama invited them to stay for dinner and was genuinely disappointed when Beth refused.

"Please, can we stay a little while longer?" Carol pleaded.

"Sorry, honey, maybe next time. I need to get home, make dinner for Daddy, and get things ready for work tomorrow."

I hated to say goodbye and see the end of our perfect day. "Mama, do they have to go?" I asked.

Mama smiled. "Beth, if it's okay with you, I wouldn't mind if Carol spends the night with Angela. That is, if she wants to," she added, giving Carol a wink.

Beth thought about it for a moment, then asked Carol what she thought.

Carol squealed with delight.

"I take that as a *yes*." Beth laughed.

I ran over and gave Mama a huge hug and thanked her for asking. I then hugged Beth and thanked her for allowing Carol to stay.

"Listen up, girls," Beth said. "Margret has agreed to let you girls do an overnighter, so be on your best behavior and don't make her regret her decision. Okay?"

"We won't," we chimed, and then headed toward my room, giggling with excitement. As we were leaving the room, I heard Beth tell Mama she would have her phone on her at all times should she need to call for any reason or if Carol changed her mind and wanted to come home.

"Okay, but I think she will be just fine," Mama said.

"Oh, I'm sure she will," Beth replied. "It's just that we have never been apart, so I am a little nervous about leaving her and going home without her. But then again, I guess we have to let go and let them grow up sometime, don't we?"

Williams

"That we do, Beth. I'll tell you what. The next time, maybe Angela can sleep over at your house. She has never stayed with anyone either—let alone have someone to play with."

"Sounds good to me. I hate to run, but I have to get home. I will see you tomorrow."

Before leaving, Beth came to my room to give Carol a final hug and kiss. Carol realized she didn't have her toothbrush, or pajamas, or a change of clothes.

"I bought some extra toothbrushes for just such an occasion," Mama said. "And I also bought several pairs of new pajamas for Angela, and I'm sure they will fit Carol as well."

"Well, I guess that settles that," Beth mumbled while fidgeting with her car keys.

"Relax, Beth; she'll be okay. Now you get on home and stop worrying. You can call her when you get there, and then again before bed tonight. How does that sound?"

"You're right, Margret." Beth turned and walked out the front door, got in her car, and slowly drove away.

CHAPTER 16

OUR FIRST OVERNIGHTER

Carol and I stayed in my room for several hours and then played outside until dark, catching lightning bugs and putting them in a jar, only to let them go before going inside for the night.

When we entered the living room, Mama was nowhere to be seen. Carol walked to the bottom of the stairs and started to go up.

I yelled just as she stepped on the first step. "No! We're not allowed up there."

"Why?" She asked.

"Because Mama's room and all her things are up there. She doesn't allow anyone to go upstairs, not even Grandma."

"Have you ever been up there?"

"No. Never."

"Don't you want to know what is up there?"

"Sometimes I do, but Mama gets really mad, and you don't want to see her when she is mad."

"Why? She seems nice. She's like my mom's best friend, just like you are my best friend."

"I like having a best friend. And I am glad our moms get along. But you have never seen Mama when she gets angry."

"Well, since we are best friends we are supposed to tell each other everything, and best friends shouldn't keep secrets from each other," she said as she stepped up on the next step.

"Carol, stop!" I shouted just as she took another step.

About that time, Mama walked into the room.

"What's going on here?" Mama shouted, nearly scaring us to death.

We both jumped, and Carol stood frozen, a look of fear on her face. She was about to cry when Mama smiled and spoke softly, "I have ice cream for you girls in the kitchen. We can make a sundae, a banana split, or you can have plain ice cream. So which one is it going to be?"

I had never had a sundae or a banana split, so I waited for Carol to choose.

We entered the kitchen to find all the fixings for ice cream you could think of—there were so many toppings it was hard to choose. Mama had everything set out in little bowls, all lined up in a row on the counter. There were bananas, nuts, cherries, strawberries, pineapple, caramel, chocolate sauce, and butterscotch. We decided to do a banana split. Mama liked pineapple in hers, but I didn't particularly care for it, and I don't think Carol did either. I had never even heard of a banana split. I was surprised at how good they were. I loved the mixture of the chocolate, strawberries and caramel flavors with the bananas, as well as the crunchiness of the nuts. I savored each bite as my taste buds danced with joy to each new flavor sensation. I loved the creaminess of the ice cream as it oozed over my tongue and slid down my throat. I wanted to remember how each flavor tasted and felt in my mouth. I was unsure of when or if I would ever get the chance to try it again. It depended on Mama's mood. But I didn't want to think about any of that stuff right now. Today was the best day of my life. And banana splits seemed like a perfect ending to a perfect day.

Mama went on and on about how much she liked being friends with Beth and how she hoped Carol enjoyed staying at our house. Mama totally ignored me, which was perfectly fine with me. She was always telling Carol to tell her mom about how she did this and that, and how much fun she had. I knew then that she was only trying to impress Beth.

Like I said, that was fine with me because I was reaping the benefits of her good intentions. No matter how fake they were.

We were laughing and talking about our day when suddenly everything grew eerily quiet. Carol seemed to be enjoying herself eating her ice cream and was oblivious to what was going on around her. I looked over at Mama, only to see that look in her eye that I knew all too well. Fear settled into the pit of my stomach like a rock. In that moment of stillness, as she kept her eyes locked onto mine, I understood all too well what she was trying to convey. I was in big trouble, and I knew it was a matter of time before she unleashed her fury on me. I also knew it wasn't going to be tonight, at least not while Carol was here. My stomach began to churn. Feeling queasy, my appetite was gone. I shoved my bowl forward and asked to be excused to go to the bathroom.

Mama nodded and continued talking to Carol.

I slid off my chair and ran out of the kitchen. I just had to get out of there. I turned to see Mama still talking and laughing. *I hope she chokes on her banana.*

Mama glared at me. It was as though she'd read my mind.

I quickly opened the bathroom door and stepped in. I sat on the floor, shaking with fear. I wanted to cry, but knew better. There was no way I could go back out there with red eyes from crying. So I sat there in my usual position, knees drawn to my chest, rocking back and forth until the fear subsided.

Once I gained my composure, I returned to the kitchen.

Mama had just finished cleaning up the mess we'd made and had left the room.

I was getting ready to sit down when she announced it was time for a bath and then bed, and that we could take our baths together. I was very uncomfortable doing that, but since Mama insisted, I felt I had no other choice. Carol got undressed, climbed into the tub and began playing with the toys Mama had placed in it when she drew our bath. I was hoping they would keep her preoccupied so she wouldn't notice when I got in.

I reluctantly undressed and quickly got in, trying hard to keep the scars hidden, but it was no use. There were too many of them. There was the scar from the cigarette burn on my arm, and one on my back. I had multiple scars on my thighs and back from the beatings I received on different occasions, usually with daddy's belt. It seemed to be Mama's favorite weapon of choice. She did stab me once in the leg with a fork and once in the chest with a knife. It didn't go very deep, but even so, if given a choice, I would rather be stabbed with a knife than with a fork. It's not like she made a conscious decision about it. It depended on what kind of mood she was in and what she was holding in her hands at the time she snaps.

Carol noticed the scars and began asking questions right away. I didn't know what to say. I couldn't tell her the truth, but I also didn't want to lie about it either. So I quickly changed the subject. Thank goodness, it worked. We finished our bath and got ready for bed. We lay for hours, laughing and giggling about anything and everything. Thank goodness Mama couldn't hear us upstairs, or we may have gotten in trouble.

Carol told me all about her family. Like me, she was an only child. I loved listening to the funny stories about her dad and her mom, but mostly the ones about her father. I couldn't help but wonder how different life would have been had my daddy lived. I lay there daydreaming of life with a real family, doing all the things a family does together, like Christmas and Thanksgiving dinner. I have never known what it was like to celebrate Thanksgiving with a big family—or any other holiday, for that matter. I wasn't sure if I even had any other family besides Mama and Grandma.

Carol rolled over and drifted off to sleep while I, on the other hand, lay there wide awake daydreaming of what could have been. I lay there for quite a while and finally began to fall asleep when Carol rolled back over, throwing one leg over me while her hand landed on my face. There was no way I could sleep like that. I ever so gently eased her off me, first her hand and then her leg. She rolled over, facing the other direction. She mumbled something in her sleep that I couldn't quite make out. Her breathing became slow and smooth. I knew she was once again in a deep sleep. I lay there enjoying the tranquil stillness of the night, staring out the window watching as the pale moonlight slowly crept in, falling upon the pictures we colored, giving them an eerie glow. My mind grew tired and could no longer contain another thought. My eyes were becoming heavy with sleep as I drifted off into peaceful slumber.

CHAPTER 17

THE GIFT

I awoke to a strange noise. It sounded like something whining. I wondered what it could be. I thought about waking Carol to see if maybe she could help me figure it out but decided to check it out myself. I tiptoed across the floor, opened the bedroom door slightly, and stuck my head out. After a few minutes, the sound started again. I could hear Mama on the front porch mumbling to herself, or so I thought. I shut the door as quietly as possible and ran back to bed and awoke Carol.

She yawned and stretched, and then asked sleepily, "What are you doing?"

"Shush," I said, placing my finger to my lips. "I hear something making noises outside. Do you want to help me figure out what it is?"

Carol's eyes grew wide as she sat up and looked around.

"Are you sure it's outside?" she asked, a little worried.

"I think so. It sounded like it was on the front porch, and Mama is out there with it."

About that time the whining started again. Carol smiled with excitement. "I know what that is! It sounds like a—"

Before she finished speaking, there was a knock at the bedroom door, and the sound was just on the other side. I stepped back away from the door, unsure of what was out there, but not Carol. She let out a squeal, jumped off the bed and ran to the door.

"Wait!" I yelled. "What if it's something awful?"

"It's not," she said, smiling as she jerked the door open. That's when I saw it. In walked the cutest little puppy I had ever seen. Come to think of it, it was the only one I had ever seen, except on television. It was light brown, fat and fluffy, and came straight to me. I bent down to pick it up, and it licked my face. Carol ran to pet it. We were giggling the whole time. My heart leaped in my throat when I looked up to see Mama standing in the doorway. I sat frozen. I didn't quite know what to expect, but it sure wasn't the reaction I got.

After a moment I was finally able to speak. "It was at the door, Mama. I don't know where it came from."

She stood staring for a moment. And then she smiled. "I know exactly where it came from."

"Where?" asked Carol, not taking her eyes off the puppy.

"I just got him from Old Man Sims down the road. He's a Golden Retriever. He's little now, but he will grow to be a big dog. He is all yours, Angela."

I know what I thought I heard, but I was unsure if I had heard correctly.

"Did she just say it was my puppy?" I whispered to Carol.

"Uh-huh." Carol nodded.

"Thank you so much, Mama. I love you!" I ran and wrapped my arms around her waist. She was smiling, but not at me. She was watching Carol playing with the puppy. "What do you think we should name it?" she asked her.

"I don't know. It's Angela's puppy. She should choose." She shrugged.

I thought for a second, then turned to Carol and asked if she would help me come up with a good name for it.

Mama didn't seem at all pleased. She stared blankly at Carol, who was now petting the puppy and laughing as it licked her face. I, on the other hand, began to get nervous and fidget, wondering what was going through her mind, when she smiled an awkward smile before speaking. "By the way, it's a boy, and he will need a cute boy name, but you have plenty of time to decide. Now take him outside. You will find a dog house ready and waiting for him. After that, come wash up for breakfast."

"Okie-dokie," Carol said.

I scooped him up in my arms and ran out with him. I gently placed him on the ground, and then we ran while he chased us back and forth across the yard. He kept barking and grabbing the bottom of our pajama legs. We were having so much fun that we forgot about breakfast—that was, until Mama stepped out on the porch and reminded us.

We raced toward the house, the puppy right on our heels. We ran in through the back door, shutting it behind us. The puppy wasn't one bit happy about that. He sat outside the door, whining.

Mama seemed to be getting annoyed, but never said anything.

My mind wandered to Grandma. I couldn't help to wonder how she was doing this morning. If my calculations were right, she should be home sometime next week. I couldn't wait to introduce her to my new friend and show her my new puppy.

Carol had been talking nonstop ever since she sat at the table, but I didn't hear a word she said until she spoke and said something about wishing her mother was as perfect as mine. I almost choked on my milk. Mama glared at me through those piercing evil eyes, sending a chill down my spine. I looked away to avoid further eye contact, hoping if I didn't look at her, she would get her mind on something else.

Beth met us at the hospital to pick up Carol. She said it was her day off and she was going to spend the day with her mother. Carol told me all about her grandmother and how silly she was at times. It made me miss my grandma all the more. It seemed like it was taking years rather than weeks for her to get well. I needed her to come home soon. Things were going smoothly at home, maybe a little too smoothly.

The rest of the week went by without a hitch. Mama only got upset a few times, but each time she would run upstairs. There she would stay for hours at a time, which was all right with me. I enjoyed having the downstairs to myself. I stayed outside for the most part, playing with my new puppy. It had been five days, and I still didn't have a name for him. I wanted to wait for Grandma to come home so she could help me choose a good one. I hated leaving him each day to go to the hospital, but I also missed Grandma and wanted to spend as much time with her as possible. The doctor said if she continued improving, she could come home in a couple of days. I couldn't wait to tell Carol and my puppy.

I hadn't seen or heard from Carol all week. Mama said it was because she had school. I hadn't had any schooling since Grandma went into the hospital. Not that I was complaining, mind you.

Beth was trying to talk Mama into sending me to regular school next year with Carol and all the other kids. I couldn't start this year since it was the end of the year. Just a few more weeks, and we would have the whole summer together. Then, hopefully, Mama would enroll me in regular school. I was hoping and praying that she would. I heard her on the phone with Beth telling her she would consider it.

Giddy with excitement, I wanted to share the news with someone, anyone. I ran outside and sat for a long time holding and petting my puppy and telling him all about it. I found it a huge relief to talk to him and tell him all my fears and deepest darkest secrets without worry of Mama finding out. I never knew anyone could feel such love for an animal. I'm not sure anyone could care for one as much as I did mine. He was there for me day and night, he cheered me up when I was down, he always made me smile, and he was always happy to see me, unlike Mama. I could fall off a cliff somewhere, and she wouldn't come looking or even notice I was gone unless she thought it was going to bring her attention and sympathy.

I erased the thought from my mind. Mama was good at making things worse than they were. I knew she was trying to get sympathy from Beth, and it worked. I feared what was going to happen when Beth caught on and no longer fell for her lies, and then Carol would no longer be allowed to be my friend. That was going to be a horrible day, and one I very much dreaded.

I was constantly on guard, even when I was playing and having fun. The thought was always in the back of my mind. I needed Grandma to come home soon. Another three days went by without incident. Mama was spending more and more time by herself upstairs. She had lost a significant amount of weight and was starting to feel better about herself.

My only hope was that she wouldn't go back to her old ways, but in my heart, I knew it was just a matter of time.

CHAPTER 18

GRANDMA COMES HOME

The day finally arrived. Grandma was coming home. Carol spent the night and went with us to pick her up. We sat in the back seat laughing and giggling as usual. Mama hardly spoke two words the whole trip. She was becoming more and more distant, spending time alone upstairs for longer periods each day. I recognized the signs, but didn't want to think about it. I guess I figured that if I didn't think about it, maybe it wouldn't happen. Or at least maybe things would get better. I quickly brushed those thoughts aside and tried to focus on the fact that Grandma was better and was coming home, and I had my best friend with me. Oh, if only things could stay this way.

We pulled into the driveway and parked in our usual spot. I opened the door and quickly jumped out. I wanted to find my puppy and introduce him to Grandma. I still hadn't named him; I wanted Grandma to help me with that. Carol and I raced toward the doghouse, but my puppy barked and ran to meet us. He jumped on me as I sat down, and started licking my face. Grandma knelt down beside me and got the same loving treatment.

"Well my goodness, he is such a little champ," she said, laughing.

"That's it!" I shouted. "I'll call him *Champ*. What do you think of that name?"

"I think it's a perfect name," Grandma said with a smile.

"Okay, then Champ it is. Do you like that name, boy?" I asked while patting him on the head.

He wagged his tail and licked my face.

"I think he likes it," Carol said, looking up at Grandma.

"I believe you're right," she replied.

Carol and I played outside while Grandma went to her room to rest and Mama started lunch. I never realized how good Mama's cooking was until now. I was usually so hungry that I ate so fast I hardly tasted anything. Whatever she was making sure smelled wonderful. The aroma filled the air, causing my stomach to respond with a little growl. At least I thought it was low until Carol began to giggle. We both started to laugh as hers began to growl also. We pretended they were talking to each other. We were always doing silly things like that, but that is what made her so fun and why we were such good friends.

As our friendship grew over the summer, so did my trust in her. One day while playing we walked down to the creek behind the house and a short distance in the woods. Just as I started to cross, I slipped and fell in the water, getting my clothes soaking wet. I was terrified of what Mama would do to me if I went home like that. In a panic, I stripped down to my panties and hung my clothes over a tree branch to dry. Once again, Carol noticed the scars and asked about them. I now felt more at ease about telling her the truth.

After making sure she wouldn't tell anyone by pinky swearing—something Carol taught me—I began from as far back as I could remember and told her everything up until right before Grandma went into the hospital. She listened wide-eyed without saying a word until I finished. She then looked at the burn scars on my back and my arm. I told her how they got there and also the stab wound. Thank goodness the scars on my legs were slowly fading. I wasn't sure if they were going away as I grew or if it was due to the tan I was getting from wearing the dress Grandma made for me. I didn't care what the reason was; I was just glad they were disappearing.

Carol grew very silent and refused to make eye contact with me. I wondered if I'd made a huge mistake. Fear began to set in, causing my heart to race. I begged her not to tell, explaining to her what would happen if Mama found out I said anything. She promised she would keep my secret by pinky swearing once again.

The feeling of relief overrode the fear. I felt more relaxed and freer now that I was able to confide in someone. I shared things with Carol that no one knew, not even Grandma. I didn't like keeping things from Grandma, but after seeing the fear and hurt in her eyes the day she caught Mama beating me broke my heart. I made up my mind then and there that I would never tell Grandma just how bad things really were. I never wanted to see fear or hurt in her eyes ever again. Mama's words played over and over in my head. "What you don't know won't hurt you." I must admit I was starting to believe that. Even though I believed those words, Grandma's words were even stronger. She always said, "Some secrets are not worth keeping, especially when they are filled with lies and alibis." I wasn't quite sure what it meant, but it sounded like wise advice, so I memorized those words.

A couple of hours later, my clothes were still damp but dry enough to wear. We walked a little further into the woods and came upon a fallen log. We sat down to rest and watched as two squirrels playfully chased one another, jumping from branch to branch, running down the tree trunk only to dart back up as quickly as they came down. We watched as they ran up the trunk, circling around and around it as they went. I heard a noise behind me and turned to see a deer slowly walking through the woods, stopping occasionally to nibble at something it found along its journey.

I sneezed, and sent the squirrels scampering off. The deer jumped and ran a short distance farther into the woods before stopping and cautiously looking around. Carol looked down in time to see something scurrying across the ground next to her feet and into the log on which we were sitting. She screamed and jumped up, causing me to do the same. We began to laugh when we saw that it was only a mouse. Neither of us wanted anything to do with a mouse.

We started walking back toward the house. I checked my clothes as we were walking. Good, they are almost dry, I thought to myself. As we approached the house, I realized Champ hadn't followed us into the woods. I called for him, but he was nowhere to be found. I ran to check his doghouse, but he wasn't in it. Carol and I both called for him as we ran around the house.

Grandma came out on the front porch just as I came around the corner. "Angel, honey what's wrong?"

"Grandma, have you seen Champ?" I asked, my eyes welling with tears.

"No, baby, I haven't seen him, but I heard him whining earlier. Now, don't you fret. He's around here somewhere."

"Will you help me look for him?" I asked.

"I sure will," she replied.

Just as she started down the steps, we heard Champ whining. He must have heard us coming, because he began barking. We hurried around the house only to find him stuck underneath it, digging at the door of my secret hiding place. Carol found us in time to see Grandma closing the entrance back and securing it.

"What is that? Is that a secret door?" she asked curiously.

Grandma and I looked at each other and immediately knew what we had to do.

"Carol, if I tell you another big secret, do you promise not to tell anyone, especially Mama?" I asked nervously.

"I promise," came her excited reply.

"Wait! Let me check to see where your mama is," Grandma said. "I'll try to keep her busy while you show Carol our little secret." She headed toward the back door of the house.

"Okay, Carol, I am about to show you something very secret. No one knows about this but me and Grandma. You can't tell your mom or anybody. Do you promise not to tell anyone?"

"Yes, yes, I promise I won't tell." She jumped up and down.

"Okay, then," I said as I slid the door over, revealing the entrance to my secret hiding place. Carol watched, but seemed unimpressed by it all. That is until I led her underneath the house and into my little spot.

"This is it," I said, looking around. "Grandma made it for me. When things get bad, and I need a place to hide, this is where I come."

"Wow!"

I had forgotten how big it was; the blanket was still lying where I had left it. Carol immediately began making plans for helping me decorate the place. The more she talked about it, the more excited we both became. I could hardly wait to get started.

CHAPTER 19

SECRET HIDING PLACE

Champ didn't take too kindly to being shut out. He began whining and scratching at the door. When that didn't work, he started barking and jumping up on the side of the house. We didn't want Mama to hear him, so we hurried out as fast as we could, opened the door and let him in. He lay in the cool dirt and slept while we worked on cleaning and figuring out how we could sneak stuff in to make it look more like a playhouse. Our mind made up, we got Champ and slipped back out, carefully closing the door and securing it shut.

By now I figured it was lunch time, so we went to check and see what we were having. The house was still and quiet as we entered. Grandma was in her room working on something. We walked into the kitchen. Mama was nowhere to be found. I knew she must be upstairs again and couldn't help but wonder what she was doing up there all this time. Carol must have been wondering the same thing, because she walked back into the living room and stood staring up the staircase.

"Don't even think about it," I told her.

"Why?" she asked, not taking her eyes off the stairs.

"Because, if you do, Mama will beat me. What do you think she would do to me for going upstairs when she told me not to?"

"I don't know, but I want to know what's up there. Don't you?"

"Yes, I do wonder what's up there, but I'm more afraid of what Mama would do to me than I am about seeing what is there. Come on, let's go see what Grandma is doing." I grabbed her by the hand and led her away from the stairs. I knew if I didn't change the subject and get her mind off it, she was going to get us both in trouble.

We knocked on Grandma's bedroom door and waited. She took longer than usual to answer. I was beginning to wonder why and what she was doing when she yelled for us to come in. I looked around, trying to figure out what she was up to. I didn't see anything out of the ordinary, so I thought she might have been lying down and resting.

Carol immediately started asking questions about the upstairs and if Grandma had ever been up there. After a brief pause, she told us that she had never thought about it before, but she had never actually been up there and never had a reason to be. I could tell right away that she was wondering herself why

Mama was so secretive about it, so much so that she would shake with anger when she was questioned about it. I explained this to Carol and begged her to not ever to go up there or ask questions. I still felt a little uneasy, even though she promised she would never bring it up again.

Grandma could no longer contain her excitement about something. She called us over to the closet and opened it to reveal two beautiful identical pink sleeveless dresses, one for me and one for Carol. We squealed with excitement as she handed them to us and told us to try them on. They were a perfect fit. We hugged Grandma to let her know how much we loved them and her for taking the time to make them for us. We also loved the fact that we felt like twins—we even pretended to be sisters.

Grandma went to the kitchen to make lunch while we sat on the front porch swing. Champ joined us. I helped him on the swing, and he licked my face as if to say *thank you*. I thought about how perfect this day was. I had my two best friends here with me, and Grandma was home. It didn't matter to me whether Mama was home or not.

I made up my mind that after Carol went home, I was going to avoid her altogether and not ask her to come back to stay. It was the only way I could protect her from Mama's rage—and save me from embarrassment. I was going to miss my friend. A deep sadness washed over me. But I also knew I had no other choice. I still had Champ and Grandma. Right now, they were the only ones I needed to focus on protecting. Unlike

Carol, I couldn't ignore them or make them go away, nor did I want to.

Mama finally emerged. I was shocked at her haggard appearance. She looked as though she hadn't slept in days; her hair was a mess and her face worn. She was wearing the same clothes she'd worn the day before. I was afraid to ask what was wrong; you never knew what kind of reaction you would get from her. So I decided to leave well enough alone. Maybe Grandma could talk with her and find out what was going on.

Grandma called us to eat lunch. Mama looked relieved that she didn't have to cook. We sat at the table and ate in silence. Everyone jumped upon hearing the phone ring. Mama answered it, then told Carol her mother was coming to pick her up and to be ready to go by the time she got here. Beth had to work that night, and Carol's dad was working out of town so she would be going to her grandparents for the entire weekend.

After lunch, I helped Carol gather her things. We had just finished when her mother pulled into the driveway. Mama didn't even go out to greet Beth, which was highly unusual, since she was always trying to find ways to impress her. I grew more and more concerned as the signs quickly progressed. I needed to talk to Grandma about it. We needed to figure out what we were going to do before someone got hurt. I tried all evening to get her alone, but Mama seemed to be everywhere I turned. Finally, the opportunity arrived when Grandma talked Mama into taking a long hot bath to relax her.

She reluctantly agreed, thus giving us some much-needed time to talk things out.

Neither one of us spoke until we heard the bath water running, and even then, we waited a few more minutes just to make sure. Several moments of silence passed, and then Grandma motioned for me to follow her outside. We walked to the garden, which was a good distance from the house. She then told me that she had seen all the warning signs that Mama had been giving off. I nodded in agreement. I told her that I wasn't going to ask Carol to come back until I was sure it was safe. I not only was afraid for Carol, but also for Grandma. She assured me she would be okay and not to worry, but telling someone not to worry in a situation like this was like throwing rocks at a hornets' nest, expecting them not to sting you.

We devised an escape plan for when Mama finally lost it. We both knew it was going to happen, and we were going to be prepared for when it did. We agreed that I was to run out the door and go immediately to my hiding place while Grandma tried to calm Mama down. If things got bad, Grandma would meet me at our hiding place. We planned on packing a few things a little at a time and hiding them there; we decided to start preparing right away. Deep down inside, I secretly hoped that day would hurry and arrive so I could leave with Grandma and start a new life, but I was also scared to death of what might happen on that terrible day.

I had never seen Mama look so awful. She walked around in a daze, talking to herself. She was losing a lot of weight, and spending countless hours alone upstairs, only to come down looking frazzled and worn. At that point, I made up my mind that I was going to find out what she was hiding up there. All I could do was hope and pray that she didn't catch me. I knew I couldn't tell Grandma about my plans; there was no way she would go along with it.

Over the next few days, we started slowly sneaking things into a duffle bag. Grandma said it would be best to put in clothes only for now, and then add snacks last, or the rats might smell it and chew everything up.

Mama grew worse as the days progressed. She was extremely withdrawn. She no longer talked to or about Beth. She ignored her phone calls until Beth finally stopped calling altogether. I still talked to Carol on the phone from time to time. I finally told her everything that was going on and why I hadn't asked her to come over. She took the news better than I expected. I then told her of my plans to go upstairs and find out what Mama was hiding. I was very excited, yet nervous at the same time. She asked if she could come over and check it out with me. I told her she couldn't, which upset her so much that she hung up on me. I didn't bother calling her back, because I knew that is what she wanted me to do, and then I would end up giving in. I just couldn't do that. I could never forgive myself if something bad happened to her. I could only hope and pray she would still talk to me once everything was over.

CHAPTER 20

FIRST DAY OF SCHOOL

As summer ended, much to everyone's surprise, Mama decided to enroll me in public school. When we walked into Ivy Dale Elementary, I was amazed at how big the place was. We followed the signs that led us to the principal's office. We were greeted by a woman who introduced herself as Mrs. Casto, the school secretary. She was an older lady with short, snow white hair. I couldn't tell what she was wearing other than a cream-colored blouse, since she remained seated behind her desk. Mama told her she was there to enroll me in school. She made a phone call and then asked us to have a seat and Mr. Deitz, the principal, would be with us shortly.

A few minutes later, Mr. Deitz stepped out of his office and asked us to come in and have a seat; he motioned toward two empty chairs in front of his desk. He closed the door and walked around and began tidying it up a bit. After placing a few papers in his desk drawer, he looked up and asked if he could help us.

Mama handed him some papers as she explained that Grandma had homeschooled me and I had never been to a public school. She said she would very much like to enroll me in the third grade; after all, I was eight years old, and that was the grade I was being homeschooled in.

Mr. Deitz quietly listened until Mama finished talking. He cleared his throat and then informed her that I would need to take some tests to see what grade level I was. I figured Mama would get upset, but she said she understood and for them to do whatever they had to do to get me in school.

I sat quietly staring at Mr. Deitz. He wore a gray suit, a white button-up shirt, and a red and gray-striped tie. His hair was black with gray throughout and was thinning on top. I couldn't quite tell how old he was, but I figured he must be older than Mama but younger than Grandma, which would put him in his mid-forties.

They took me to a room and introduced me to a teacher, whom I liked a lot. Her name was Mrs. Garrison, but she said I could call her Mary as long I didn't tell the other kids. I chose to call her Mrs. Garrison just like everyone else. She was slim and beautiful with straight black hair she parted to one side. Her makeup was perfect. The colors she used accented her skin tone, making her dark brown eyes stand out all the more. She wore a black skirt that hung just above her knees, a dark green button-up blouse, and black high heels. I wondered how she walked in those things. I told her I thought she was very pretty. She smiled and then said she thought I was very pretty as well. No one had ever said that—I mean, other than Grandma, but I figured Grandmas are supposed to say stuff like that.

She sat me down at a small table and began my exam. She told Mama that it would be a while, so if she had things she needed to do she could come back and pick me up later. At first, she refused, but after a few minutes, she decided she had errands to run after all, and I was relieved she decided to leave. Testing went much faster without her there.

After testing was over, Mrs. Garrison gave me a tour of the school and showed me my classroom. As we walked in, I heard someone squeal with delight and yell my name. I turned to see Carol sitting at a desk in the third row. She was smiling and bouncing in her seat and whispered to the girl seated next to her that I was her best friend. The teacher, Mrs. Blake, was short and chubby with an oval shaped face. Her blond hair was pulled back into a ponytail; she wore gray dress pants, a red shirt, and black high-heel boots. I thought she was charming. She had me to turn and face the class while she introduced me.

"Class, I would like you all to give a warm welcome to our newest student. Sorry, dear, but what was your name again?" she asked, smiling.

"Angela, but my grandma calls me Angel," I said excitedly. I was so happy to be there with kids my age.

"Okay, sweetie. Which name do you prefer?"

"I like Angel, but Angela will do just fine, thank you."

"Oh my, she's such a polite child," she said to Mrs. Garrison.

Several kids in class started calling me by name. A little girl on the front row named Molly yelled, "Sit by me, Angela!"

Then another girl across the room shouted, "No! You can sit by me."

Carol spoke up and said, "She is my friend and is sitting by me."

A boy named Timmy yelled that she could sit where she wanted.

"Shut up, Timmy, and mind your own business," Carol yelled.

The class began to snicker. Timmy didn't appear at all happy about having been spoken to that way.

"All right, class, settle down." Mrs. Blake turned to Mrs. Garrison. "Will Angela be staying with us today?"

"I don't think so," Mrs. Garrison answered. "We need to wait for the results of her exam before we know which grade, she should be placed in."

Mama and the principal stepped into the room. The class began to chant in unison. "Let . . . her . . . stay . . . . Let . . . her . . . stay."

"Quiet, please," Mrs. Blake insisted.

"Margret? Mrs. Angela's Mom?" Carol said. "Can Angela stay, just for today? See what school's like?"

The principal glanced at Mama, then nodded. "That sounds like a good way to get used to the way things worked around here." He looked again at Mama, his eyebrows raised.

With my fingers crossed, I waited for her reply.

"Yes," she finally said. "Angela can stay."

The classroom exploded in applause.

After a few seconds, Mr. Deitz motioned for everyone to quiet down. "Well, it looks as though everyone agrees and wants you to stay. What do you think, little lady?"

I smiled. "Yes. Please."

I took the seat next to Carol, and she showed me what kind of work they were doing. I was surprised to see that it was stuff that Grandma had already taught me. I don't know what I expected it to be like in school, but it didn't seem much different than working at home, except I would be with other kids my age. When the class started on worksheets, I asked if I could have one too.

The teacher seemed thrilled as she handed me one. She told me to do whatever I could and not to worry about the stuff I didn't understand. I wasn't sure why she would say that. I found the work to be very easy.

She sure looked surprised when I handed her back the completed worksheet before the rest of the class finished. She was even more surprised when she checked it, and I had gotten all the answers right. She then left the room with my worksheet in hand.

After giving Carol all the answers, I thought it only fair to help the rest of the class. I picked up a worksheet off the desk and stood and announced my plans to the class. Everyone started getting loud and anxious for the answers. Molly jumped up to calm them down.

"Everyone be quiet," she said in a low voice. "You heard Miss Blake. We can't go out for recess until our worksheets are finished."

"Well, if she gives the answers, I'm telling," Marylou yelled from the back of the room.

Carol stood and yelled back at her, "If you don't want to know the answers, then cover your ears. And if you tell, I will punch you in the nose."

Marylou's expression turned from sarcasm to worry. She didn't speak another word as I stood and told the class the answers. I had just sat back down when Miss Blake returned to the room.

"Okay, class, settle down. Angela, I need you to come with me, please. Jessica, I need you to take over class until I get back."

Jessica sat behind me and was the tallest girl in class—she was even taller than the boys. She was a pretty girl with long straight brown hair that hung to her hips. She leaned forward in her seat and tapped me on the shoulder. "Good luck," she whispered.

I nodded as I stood and nervously followed Miss Blake out of the room. *She must have heard me telling the class the answers.* I wasn't sure what was going to happen now, especially if she called Mama. We walked down the hallway. I wasn't quite sure where she was taking me, but I figured it had to be to the principal's office. It had to be something terrible. Carol once told me that if you ever get called out of the room and taken to the principal's office, it's not a good sign.

"Am I in trouble?" I asked.

"No, you're not in trouble," she said with a smile. "We just need to do a few more tests.

"What kind of tests?" I asked nervously.

"Oh, just some tests to see how smart you are."

"Why do they need to know that?" I asked.

"Because if you are as smart as I think you are, they will move you to a higher-grade level."

"Will I still get to be in your class?"

"No. They will move you to a different level, but your teacher will be nice."

I pondered that for a moment, then told her I didn't want to move to a higher grade; I liked the class I was in just fine. She smiled and said that I needed to be in a class that wasn't too easy for me, one that would be more of a challenge. I asked her what would happen if I failed the test. She smiled sweetly and informed me that I was to do my very best to pass, adding that if I didn't, I would be stuck in the third grade all year and how it was an honor to get double promoted.

I knew what I had to do. I had to fail that test. I didn't want to be double promoted. I wanted to be in a class with kids my age, a class with my best friend. I just wanted to be like all the other children and have a normal life.

We turned the corner and started down the long hallway that led to the principal's office. I kept my head down and watched the floor as we walked, trying not to step on a crack just like Carol taught me one day while playing at the hospital. The beige colored tiles looked wet, even though they weren't. I wondered how they kept them so shiny. I noticed Miss Blake's high heel shoes. I loved the click-clacking sound they made on the hard floor. I thought she was a beautiful lady. Her smile made me feel good.

I glimpsed through the window in each classroom door as we passed. Although I could see and hear the teachers as they taught their classes, neither the teachers nor the students seemed to notice us.

As we entered the outer office, I was directed to sit and wait, just as before. Miss Blake walked into the principal's office and explained why she had brought me there. I could hear them talking, but couldn't quite make out what they were saying. After a few moments, she stepped back into the room and led me into the small room on the left, the same one I had taken the tests in earlier. I hated taking those tests, but this time I looked forward to getting them out of the way so I could get back to the classroom and the other students, especially Carol.

Another teacher entered the room. He couldn't have been much older than Miss Blake. He introduced himself as Mr. Conley. His glasses appeared too big for his face, and he was always pushing them back up on the bridge of his nose. He asked me a lot of questions before giving the test. I made sure to miss several of them purposely. I finished as quickly as possible and then asked if I could go back to the classroom.

Miss Blake asked if I remembered where it was. I nodded and said room 10. She told me to go ahead, and she would be there in a few moments. I hurried back to the classroom as fast as my feet could carry me—without running, of course. Carol jumped out of her seat and ran to meet me along with a few other students. They began asking questions faster than I could answer.

"What happened?" asked Carol.

"I had to—"

"She got in trouble. What do you think happened?" Molly said in her usual sarcastic tone.

"Well, actually—" I started, but was cut off once again by another student.

"Shut up and let her answer," Carol yelled.

Once everyone quieted down, I told them what had happened and how I failed my test on purpose so I could stay in the class with them.

Molly stood and yelled from across the room, "I'm telling."

I'd had enough of Molly. As I marched over to her, my first instinct was to punch her in the nose, but Grandma's words kept playing over and over in my mind. "Don't fight unless you absolutely have no choice. If possible, talk your way out, and sometimes, you might even make a friend out of whom you first saw as an enemy."

I didn't want to be friends with someone like her, but I also didn't want to get into trouble for fear that Mama would get mad and take me out of school. I stood over her, looking her in the eyes. I could see she was worried, unsure of what I was going to do, and took a step back.

I looked down and then very sweetly said, "Wow! Molly, I love your dress. It's beautiful."

That was all it took. Molly looked down, held her dress out at each side, and twisted back and forth.

"Do you really like it?" she asked with a smile.

"Yes, it's beautiful, and pink is my favorite color."

"Thank you," Molly replied. "My mother bought it for me at Brown's Department store, and it cost a lot of money," she said smugly.

"Well, they sell good stuff then." It was all I could think to say, but it seemed to please Molly enough to take her mind off telling on me.

"Do you want to play with us at playtime?" I asked, motioning toward Carol and a few other girls across the room.

"It's called a recess, and I would like that very much." Her eyes lit up.

It was then I realized that she had no real friends at all. I felt sorry for her. . She sat down upon seeing Miss Blake enter the room.

"Okay, class, take your seats and settle down."

Everyone took their seats. I looked over at Molly, who was still smiling and admiring her new dress. I knew then what Grandma meant, and she was right. I avoided getting into a fight which would have resulted in my getting into trouble, and then Mama getting upset and forcing me to be homeschooled. Don't get me wrong, homeschool has its advantages, such as sleeping in later and being taught by Grandma, but there were no other kids around to play with. I enjoyed my time with Grandma—she was a loving and patient teacher—but I really enjoyed being taught in a classroom along with other students more.

I kept my word and played with Molly along with Carol and a few others during recess. Even though Carol protested at first, she finally saw things my way after I explained my reasons, and we had a wonderful time. Upon returning to the classroom, Mr. Deitz met me at the door and told me to wait in the hallway. He waited for Miss Blake to get the class settled, and then she joined us.

"It's official. You will attend public school," Mr. Deitz said.

I could hardly wait to tell Grandma I would be going to school with my best friend. I was so happy and gave them both Mr. Deitz and Miss Blake a big hug. They smiled and sent me back to class.

When I told Carol what they said, she jumped out of her seat, and we hugged as we jumped up and down in place, giggling with excitement. We sat down when Miss Blake stepped back into the room wearing a huge grin. She appeared to be just as happy for me as Carol was.

The rest of the day went by quickly. I didn't want to leave, but knew I would be returning tomorrow. I smiled as I got on the bus for the first time. I took my seat with Carol at the back of the bus. It felt strange. My legs were too short to reach the floor; they felt weird dangling as I bounced up and down with every bump. I enjoyed it, and Carol was right, it was fun, and I loved it.

My first year of school went by quickly. I loved the idea of getting promoted with the rest of the class and continuing to the next grade with everyone, and I realized I was the only one who enjoyed the first day of school and hated the last. I loved being at school.

CHAPTER 21

CHAMP TO THE RESCUE

The next few years came and went. I was now in fifth grade—ten years old—and school would be out in a few weeks. Oh, how I hated to see it end. I couldn't imagine what summer was going to be like, now that I would spend my days with Mama and all her weird mood swings, which had grown increasingly worse with each passing year. Hopefully, I would be spending a lot of time with Carol, and when I wasn't with her, I could keep myself busy playing with Champ or helping Grandma in her garden.

The following weeks flew by quickly. School was out, and once again I was stuck on the mountain. I stayed out of Mama's hair, and thus stayed out of trouble. I had a good summer. Mama had her good days as well as some bad. Grandma tried once again to get her help, but to no avail. Each time she tried, she always ended up looking like the crazy person, thanks to Mama and all her lies. Grandma grew tired of trying to find someone who would believe her, so she finally gave up.

Summer quickly turned into fall. It was now October and my eleventh birthday was a week away—not that it mattered, because Mama never celebrated it.

Grandma, on the other hand, always tried to do a little something with me to make it a special day. I was glad I was born during this time of the year, because fall is one of my favorite seasons. Along with it came colder weather and the changing of the leaves. The trees and brush are painted the most beautiful, breathtaking colors. I loved getting up early in the mornings just to watch the sun rise over the mountains. We were surrounded by them on every side. When the sunlight hit the mountains just right, the red, gold and orange leaves blended, making them appear as though they were on fire; yet, everything seemed so serene. I felt as though I didn't have a care the world. But that didn't last long. I was brought back to reality upon hearing Mama's footsteps descending the stairs. I cringed at the thought of her being up so early. That meant only one thing. Today was going to be a bad day.

I quietly moved away from the window and climbed back into bed, pulling the covers over my head, and lay there silently praying she wouldn't come into my room. I breathed a sigh of relief as her footsteps moved toward the kitchen. Swinging my legs over the side of the bed, I sat for a moment, trying to decide what I should do. Should I get up and see if she needed help and risk dealing with one of her angry outbursts? Or should I stay in bed and hope she was in a better mood later in the morning? I decided to stay in my room.

Even though my room stayed spotless, I was hoping that if I made my bed, cleaned and dusted without being told, she might get in a better mood. I knew I was only fooling myself when I opened my bedroom door and listened as Mama talked and even argued with someone who wasn't there.

She was worse than ever. I managed to avoid her, but then again, it wasn't that hard since she was still spending most of her time upstairs. She had lost so much weight her clothes were hanging off her. Grandma was the only one who could get through to her, except when she had an angry outburst—which was now more often.

I kept myself busy with other things, anything to stay out of the house and away from her. When she flew into a rage, I would quietly slip out, make my way to the side of the house, and hide in my secret hiding place. I would stay there until Grandma came to get me, or until I felt it was safe to come out. There was no question about it. Mama needed professional help.

It was Tuesday, and school let out early due to a broken water pipe or something. I didn't tell the teacher that nobody answered the phone when I called to let them know that I would be home early. So I wasn't surprised when there was no one there to pick me up at the bus stop. A few minutes into my long walk home, Old Man Sims pulled up alongside me in his old pickup truck. It was dark green and appeared to be on its last leg. He offered me a ride. I smiled and thanked him as I climbed in the back. It was hard to find a clean place to sit, with all the junk he had piled in there. There was garbage everywhere All kinds of beer cans, empty food containers from fast food restaurants, empty soda cans, tools thrown here and there, and a lot of bicycle parts, which reminded me that I had never had a bike, let alone learned to ride one. As we drove up the road, now and then I would catch the faint scent of something rotten. I assumed it was coming from the back of the truck. I couldn't tell exactly where it was coming from and didn't want to know.

It was a bumpy ride, but a ride none the less, and one I gladly accepted. I sat quietly watching the trees become a blur as we passed. The truck stirred up dust on the old dirt road, and I watched as it began to settle behind us. I caught a glimpse of a deer running in front of us and through the woods. She ran a short distance before stopping and turning to stare as we drove past. The ride didn't take as long as I imagined it would. As the old pickup rolled to a stop in front of his house, I jumped out and thanked him for the ride. He merely nodded, a slight smile crossing his face before pulling into his driveway.

I noticed he had been doing some work around his place. I complimented him on how much better it looked. He smiled and said he figured it was time to whip things back into shape. I offered to help anytime should he need me. He thanked me for the offer and said he would keep that in mind. I waved goodbye and began walking toward home.

"Angel!" Mr. Sims hollered.

"Yes, sir?" I turned to face him.

"Now that you mentioned it, I could use some help with the animals." He nodded toward the dogs, who stood with their ears perked as though they understood every word. "That is, if you wouldn't mind helping with them."

"Yes! I mean, I would love that, but only if I can bring Champ?"

"Well, now, I reckon that would be okay." He smiled and ran his fingers through his thinning gray hair. "If it's all right with your mother, you can start tomorrow."

"Would you mind calling Mama and asking her if it's okay?"

"Sure, just jot down the number and I will call her in a little while." He bent down and patted one of the small dogs on top of the head.

I retrieved a pencil and piece of paper from my bookbag and wrote the number down. "Here ya go." I held it out and waited for him to take it.

He stretched out his hand and gently took it. "Thank you. I will pay you for your trouble. That is, if you are allowed to work for me."

"You don't have to pay me anything. I volunteer." I grinned.

"No, ma'am, you're not working for free. My conscience won't allow it. By the way, this here is Bentley." He picked up the little dog and turned him to face me. "I'll introduce you to the rest of them later."

"Okay. Hope to see you tomorrow." I waved goodbye and started walking toward home.

"I could drive you home, if you like," Old Man Sims shouted over the barking dogs.

I turned to look at him while walking backwards. "Thanks, but I would much rather walk," I replied.

He simply nodded and tossed a stick for Bentley to fetch.

I took my time walking home.

The surroundings were beautiful and peaceful; everything was quiet except for the occasional chatter of chipmunks. I imagined they were chirping out a song to their one true love or instructions to the others, as they prepared for the long winter ahead.

I loved how the leaves fell from the trees like snowflakes, slowly drifting down. Some spun and twirled, while others swayed back and forth, making their way down and then gently landing on the ground. I wondered what it would be like to be a leaf, breaking free, not knowing or caring where I would land, enjoying the ride and going wherever the wind blew me. As much as I loved watching the falling leaves, I also dreaded the thought of the coming winter. Winter meant more time cooped up in the house with Mama. I was so lost in thought I didn't hear the car pull up behind me. I jumped when the horn blew. I turned and was relieved to see Beth and Carol. Beth hadn't visited Mama in months, and I tried keeping my visits with Carol limited to school only. Seeing them both filled my heart with joy. I was hoping their visit might cheer Mama up some, or at least bring her back to reality. It would be nice to have her the way she was when she first met Beth and was bending over backwards trying to impress her.

Carol scooted over, and I sat down beside her in the front seat. She immediately began talking about my upcoming birthday and asked if I were going to have a party. She looked surprised when I told her I had never had a party, and figured Mama wasn't going to start by giving me one now.

"Mom, can we give her a party?" Carol asked, a little apprehensively.

"Well, honey, we will talk to her mother, and if she says it's all right, then we will see what we can do."

Carol and I squealed in unison.

"Okay, girls, calm down." Beth laughed. "We don't know if her mother has plans of her own, so don't get too excited about it."

Champ would have come running to meet us as we pulled into the driveway had he not been chained to his doghouse. It had been months since Carol last saw him.

"Oh my goodness, I can't believe how big he has gotten," Carol said. "I wonder if he remembers me."

"I'm sure he does. He's a smart dog," I said.

We got out of the car and ran toward Champ, who was barking and lunging on his chain. He jumped on me and almost knocked me down, and then started licking my face. Mama despised that habit and insisted I break him of it. I promised her I would work on it. But I loved the feeling of knowing someone other than Grandma was happy to see me come home. I didn't think I could care for anyone as much as I loved Grandma, but Champ proved me wrong. Now I couldn't imagine life without him. I let him loose, and Carol got the same welcome.

"I told you he would remember you."

"You're right—he is a smart dog." She patted him on the head.

Carol and I played outside with Champ while Beth disappeared inside to talk with Mama It wasn't long before they reappeared. Beth told Mama she would call her later and they could work out the details for the party. Carol and I hugged goodbye before she left. They got in their car and started down the driveway. Mama stood at the top of the steps smiling and waving until they were out of sight. It was nice to see her smiling again.

I continued to play fetch with Champ, which happened to be his favorite game. I threw the ball and watched it roll across the grass. Champ got to it before it even stopped moving. Then he would run back and lay it at my feet. He never grew tired of playing. I decided to throw the ball farther so that he wouldn't make it back as quickly. Just as I threw it, I felt someone grab my arm, jerk me around and slap me across the face. I stumbled backward and hit flat on my back on the ground. I looked up to see Mama standing over me. Before I could say anything, she grabbed me by the arm and pulled me up to my feet. Her fist was clenched by her side, so I knew she was going to punch me.

She was mumbling something about me telling Beth I'd never had a birthday party. The angry expression on her face and the look in her eyes frightened me. I covered my face with my free hand, and I closed my eyes, awaiting the awful blow. I peeked just as she drew back to punch me in the face Champ lunged at her, knocking her to the ground, and then stood over her, his hair standing up on his back, teeth bared and growling fiercely. I had never heard him do that before. We were both taken by surprise. I just stood there, staring, not knowing what to do.

For once it was my Mama on the ground, with her hand over her face and fear in her eyes.

"Angela! Call off your dog," she said, trying to stay calm.

I was so shocked that it took a moment to sink in what she was asking me to do. So when I didn't move right away, she grew angrier.

"Angela! I said for you to call Champ off *now*!"

With that, Champ took a step forward. He was now almost nose to nose with her, growling more fiercely than before.

This time I saw more than just fear in her eyes. It was a look of pure terror.

"No, Champ!" I yelled, grabbing him by his collar and pulling back on him. At first, I didn't think he was going to listen to me. I could see the hatred in his eyes. I had no idea why he hated her so much. I had never even seen her pet him. I looked around and saw the ball he had retrieved earlier. I slowly bent down and picked it up.

"Here, Champ, look what I have. Do you want to play?" I held up the ball. "Fetch!" I yelled as I threw it into the backyard. Forgetting all about what had just happened, he ran off to fetch the ball. In the meantime, Mama got to her feet, pulled down her t-shirt, and then tried to wipe the grass stain off her blue jeans. She was shaking like a leaf and still extremely angry.

"If that dog ever tries that again, he is gone," she said in a low voice while keeping an eye on Champ at the same time.

I looked over to see Champ playfully chasing a few birds. They would fly a short distance, and he would run after them again and again. I couldn't help to smile.

"Angela! Do I make myself clear?" Anger arose in her voice once again.

Champ stopped what he was doing and turned our way. I secretly patted my leg, which was his signal to come. When Mama saw Champ heading toward us at a slow run, she decided it was time to go in the house. She stopped on the porch, and before going in, she yelled, "I mean it, Angela. If that dog ever tries that again, he is out of here."

Williams

"Yes, ma'am," I said without looking at her. She turned and marched into the house, slamming the door shut behind her. My full attention was on Champ, who was now by my side licking my hand. Reaching into my pocket, I pulled out a cookie I had saved from my school lunch. I fed it to him, all the while patting him on the head and telling him what a good boy he was and how proud I was of him for protecting me. I leaned down and gave him a big hug. "I love you, Champ, and I will always take care of you," I whispered in his ear. He licked my face as though he understood.

I stayed outside the rest of the day. I didn't dare step foot in the house. I knew better than to be anywhere alone with Mama. Grandma's friend Bonnie pulled into the driveway and dropped her off. I ran to meet her. I had thought about telling her what had happened earlier, but when I saw Mama watching from a window, I decided it was best to wait.

"How was your quilting class, Grandma?" I asked.

"We didn't have quilting class. We went shopping, and I bought you a surprise." That's when I realized she was holding several bags.

"Oh, wow! Did you just say you have a surprise for me? What is it? Can I see?" I reached for one of the bags.

"Not so fast." She laughed while placing it behind her back. "It wouldn't be a surprise if I told you what it was, now, would it?"

"I guess not," I said, trying to sound disappointed, but what was actually on my mind was what had just happened with

Champ. Looking at the window, I noticed that Mama was no longer there.

"Grandma, I have something important to tell you," I whispered.

"What is it?" A look of concern replaced her smile.

"I can't tell you now, but it's about Champ."

"Okay, we will talk about it later then," she whispered back.

I took one of the bags and followed her into the house and the kitchen. She looked around, and then asked where Mama was. Before I could answer, we heard movement coming from upstairs. I smiled and pointed at the ceiling.

"How was school today?" She put away a few groceries and then handed me a chocolate bar. I told her all about my day at school and the birthday party Beth and Carol were going to throw for me.

"What were you trying to tell me about Champ?" she asked.

"Oh, yeah, I almost forgot," I said. Grandma silently listened while I told her everything from the beginning to the end with how Champ protected me.

Her reflective gaze searched my face and her brow furrowed with concern. "Angel, honey, listen to me," she said in a stern voice. "From now on, you need to make sure Champ is kept out of sight as much as possible, and tie him up before you go to bed at night. It's imperative that you do this every night from now on. As a matter of fact, it may be best to keep him tied up at all times. Do you understand?"

I nodded. I understood all too well. Tying him up would keep him out of Mama's hair and thus out of trouble. Champ protected me from Mama, and now it was my turn to protect him from her. I knew she meant what she said about getting rid of him; I just hoped she would forget about what happened, even though deep down I knew it was never going to happen.

I did as Grandma said and kept Champ out of sight. I tied him up while I was in school, but when I was home, I would take him into the woods to play. He loved it, and always managed to find a rabbit or squirrel to chase. I loved watching him chase the little birds as they landed in the field. I wasn't sure what kind of birds they were, and Champ didn't seem to care. He loved running and jumping in the middle of them. They would fly up into the air a short distance and then land several feet away. It seemed as though they were teasing him, daring him to chase them. They had created their own little game. I often wondered what crossed their minds— and also Champ's, for that matter. This game continued until the birds grew tired or flew away, or something else caught Champ's attention.

After tying Champ up, I walked up the steps that led to the back door. Mama hung up the phone just as I stepped inside.

"That was Old Man Sims." She paused. "He wants you to work for him around the house and help take care of his animals. He said he would pay you, if you want the job," she said.

"Can I, Mama?" I asked, trying not to sound too excited.

Mama stood quietly pondering it over. A few agonizing minutes later she finally answered. "Well, I suppose it wouldn't hurt for you to learn some responsibility and make a little spending money for yourself." She smiled.

"Thank you, Mama," I said calmly, when I was actually exploding on the inside. I rushed outside to Champ and let out a huge squeal of delight.

Every day after school I'd hurry home, change and then Champ and I walked the half mile down the road to work. *Work.* I loved the sound of that.

We did this every day for a few months. I enjoyed taking care of the animals. I helped bathe, groom and feed them all. I also helped clean the dog houses and the yard. I like spending time with Old Man Sim's He was funny, kind, and a welcome break from the stress at home. Champ loved it to.

I knew we wouldn't be able to do it much longer due to colder weather. I dreaded the thought. I would have to find something else to keep us busy until warmer weather. I wasn't sure which of us would be more disappointed. There had to be something we could do to occupy our time. After studying on it for a while, it hit me, and I knew just what we would do. I couldn't help but smile and feel proud of myself. Champ needed me, and I was going to protect him and take care of him.

My mind was made up. We would continue our little ritual on the warmest days and then stick to playing in the backyard on the coldest ones. I don't think it mattered to Champ where we played. He was just happy to spend time with me and to have my full attention, and I was more than happy to give it to him.

On the days Mama wasn't home, I would take him to my secret hiding place to see if he would behave himself. If he would, then we could go there on the very coldest of days. For reasons I couldn't explain, it seemed to stay warm under that part of the house.

Soon a day came when it was too cold to go outside, so I stayed in my room coloring and keeping myself busy. Something crashed outside my door. I opened the door and ran into the living room without looking or thinking. Mama had dropped a drinking glass on the floor, shattering it. I stepped on the glass, cutting both feet and getting shards of glass stuck to the bottom of them. The pain was unbearable. Unable to walk, I sat down on the floor and screamed in pain.

Mama ran to check on me. She knelt down beside me. "Angela, baby, are you all right?" she asked. "It hurts so badly," I answered between sobs. I placed my arms around her and hugged her tight, wanting her to comfort me. Her body stiffened, and she pulled away from me. I looked up at her to see what the problem was. She was staring right past me. I looked back to see what she was staring at but there was nothing there.

"Mama, are you okay?"

Her gentle, loving demeanor changed as well as the look on her face. Her eyes glazed over and turned as black as coal. She stood towering over me and began screaming and yelling at me for being stupid and not watching where I was walking. During all the commotion, Grandma ran out of her room to find out what was going on. She ran in just in time to see Mama kick me in the ribs for getting blood all over the floor and yelling that she had just mopped, and I had made a mess.

The anger in Grandma's eyes was unforgettable. "What's going on?" she shouted. "Margret, I'm talking to you!" Grandma snapped her fingers.

Mama stared blankly as though in a trance. Staggering like a drunk, she stumbled backward, knocking over the mop bucket. She then slipped on the dirty water and hit the floor, flat on her butt.

By this time Grandma was at my side, picking the shards of glass from my feet. She ran and grabbed some bandages and lovingly wrapped them. Mama sat in stunned silence, trying to figure out what had just happened. I made the mistake of looking at her.

I knew her whole backside was soaking wet from the dirty mop water, but the look on her face was priceless. I couldn't help myself, and I burst into laughter. Grandma tried to shush me, but the more she tried, the harder I laughed.

That was the final straw. Mama, fuming with anger, stood, grabbed the mop, and swung it as she was coming toward me. Grandma tried to block her from hitting me and took a hard blow to her arm just below her elbow. I heard a loud crack, and, at first, I thought the mop handle had broken, but soon realized it was Grandma's arm instead.

I guess Mama didn't notice what she had done, because she kept coming for me. The expression on her face and the look in her eyes were beyond frightening. I jumped up, full of adrenaline, and ran out the door. I wasn't sure if she was following me. I just ran for all that was in me, not looking back.

I could hear Grandma screaming that her arm was broken, and she needed to get to the hospital. It was now or never. I opened the door to my hiding place. I quickly made my way to my secret spot and lay down on the musty old blanket, burying my face into it, softly crying and praying a silent prayer for Grandma, asking God to please take care of her and let her be all right.

Several minutes later, I heard the car start and pull out of the driveway. I knew they were on their way to the hospital. I continued to lay there, crying long after they were gone until there were no tears left. I rolled onto my side and lay there staring at the wall. I could see the big maple tree through a crack in the board, with its branches stretched out far and wide like it was guarding something.

As I lay staring at it, I began to daydream that I was the one the tree was protecting, and that one-day Mama would get too close to it. It would come alive, its branches crashing down, wrapping around her, and holding her tight against its massive trunk. Then I would be the one laughing, as she begged and pleaded for it not to hurt her.

I never pictured the tree ever harming her. Even though she was cruel and heartless, I promised myself and Grandma that I would never become like her.

Several hours later, I grew bored and figured it was safe to come out. I hobbled to the front of the house. Stopping on the porch, I took off the now muddy bandages and wadded them up in my hand. I knew better than to get mud all over the floor. It was bad enough that there was broken glass and blood everywhere. I found the roll of bandages on the floor right where Grandma had left them. I picked them up and tiptoed to the bathroom. Not that I was trying to be quiet, but because my toes were the only part of my feet that weren't cut. Nevertheless, they began to bleed once again. It didn't matter, since the floor was still a mess, only now there was a trail of blood leading to the bathroom.

I climbed in the tub and washed and wrapped my feet as best I could. I got a small bag from under the bathroom sink before going back into the living room. I proceeded to clean up the broken glass, picking up the biggest pieces and placing them in the bag. I then swept the rest into the dustpan and emptied it in the bag as well. Next, I got the mop, which was still wet from when Mama used it just a few hours before. I cleaned up all the blood and then tried rinsing the mop afterward, but my hands were too small to reach around it. I squeezed out as much water as possible and put it back where I found it, and then went to my room and awaited their return.

A couple of hours later, they pulled into the driveway. I met Grandma as she was coming through the front door, and she didn't appear at all happy. Her wrist was in a cast, and she refused to speak to Mama. My mother didn't take too kindly to being ignored by anyone, especially Grandma.

"Mother, would you please just talk to me?" Mama pleaded.

To which Grandma held up her hand and shook her head. "I'm done."

"Please," Mama begged. "Give me a chance to explain?"

"Explain what? How you lied about getting rid of those books?"

Mama stood dumbfounded. I probably had the same blank look on my face. I had no idea Grandma had talked to Mama about the books.

"Don't you see what those books are doing to you?" Grandma continued. "Witchcraft is evil and dangerous. Get rid of them before something worse happens."

Without saying a word, Grandma slowly made her way to her bedroom and shut the door behind her.

Mama finally gave up, mumbled something under her breath, and then went upstairs, where she stayed for the rest of the evening.

CHAPTER 22

BIRTHDAY PARTY

The day of my eleventh birthday finally arrived. I still wasn't sure if I was having a party or not. No one had mentioned it since the day Beth visited. I started to ask Carol about it, but changed my mind. It was the first time I was anxious for school to let out. I could hardly wait to get home. I just knew that everyone would be there to surprise me.

Suddenly, a terrible thought crossed my mind. What if Mama changed her mind? It would be just like her to do that as punishment for Champ attacking her.

The feeling of dread quickly replaced the excitement I'd felt just moments earlier. Now I understood why Carol hadn't mentioned it. And I was glad I never asked. The day seemed to drag by, but I didn't mind since I was sure there was not going to be a party when I returned home. The only thing I knew for sure was that Champ would be there waiting for me.

A slight smile crossed my lips at the thought of him running to meet me—only he couldn't do that anymore, since I had to keep him tied up. He hated it just as much as I did, but like Grandma said, it was the only way of keeping him safe—at least until Mama's anger subsided, which didn't seem to be anytime soon.

School finally came to an end. I could hardly wait to get home and grab something to eat. I hadn't had much of an appetite during lunch, but now I was starving. Carol barely spoke two words to me the whole day. And I could say the same of myself. I had so much on my mind, that I hadn't thought about it until now.

Mama was in her usual parking spot when the bus dropped me off at the end of our road. I noticed that she was extremely quiet, which was unusual even for her. Don't get me wrong; I wasn't complaining. I was happy the ride up the mountain was a quiet one.

I missed the fact that Champ didn't come running to meet us as the car pulled into the driveway, but I also knew it was too soon to untie him, mainly when I wasn't home to watch him or keep him out of trouble. The first thing I did after getting out of the car was to run out back and check on him. He was just as happy to see me as I was him. He showed it the only way he knew how, by barking and trying to jump on me.

"Angela! How many times do I have to tell you to keep that dog quiet?" Mama yelled from the back door.

"Yes, ma'am," I answered without so much as looking at her; I was too busy trying to untie him so we could play awhile before it got dark.

I heard the door shut just as Champ looked her way and bared his teeth. "No, Champ, no!" I grabbed his collar and held on tight. I hated to scold him for trying to protect me, but it was for his own good. I sure didn't want Mama giving him back to Old Man Sims—or worse, to a stranger. I decided it was best to keep him tied up until I was ready to give him my full attention, even though he didn't seem to agree. He began whining and barking worse than ever as I walked away.

I went back into the house to get something to eat before taking him into the woods to play. Grandma came out of her room and asked if I wanted to ride into town with her. I wondered if Mama was coming. She said she wasn't sure, but would ask her as soon she came back downstairs.

I slipped my shoes back on and headed for the front door when I heard a noise behind me. I turned to see Mama dressed nicely in a tight-fitting pair of blue jeans and a dark blue blouse that looked good on her and showed off her new curves. She'd curled the ends of her long black hair, which she wore down for a change. I don't remember ever seeing her hair down. I gasped when I saw her.

"Wow! You look pretty, Mama."

"Thank you." She smiled, and her eyes lit up for the first time in months.

As we headed out the door, I realized this was the first trip we had made together as a family. I mentioned it to Grandma, but she never said much, she just smiled and gave a little nod. She told me to go to the car and wait for them. I did as I was told and sat in the backseat, my stomach growling. I began to wish I had eaten lunch at school. I tried to think of something else, but I couldn't get my mind off food, which made the trip go by fast. Before I knew it, we were at the bottom of the mountain and heading toward town. I had no idea where we were going; I was just glad we were doing something together like a real family. Hopefully it included stopping to get something to eat soon.

I was so happy when Mama pulled into the Pizza Place parking lot. I scooted up on the edge of my seat and tapped Grandma on the shoulder.

"Are we going in to eat?" I asked.

"Yes, we sure are." She opened the door and stepped out. I got out and could hardly wait to get inside. I was hungry as well as thirsty.

We stepped through the doors of the Pizza Place with me in the lead. The aroma of food made my stomach growl all the more. Just as we entered, there came a loud shout from inside the building. "SURPRISE!"

I nearly jumped out of my skin.

At first, I had no idea what was going on, until someone yelled, "Happy Birthday!" I turned to see Mama and Grandma grinning proudly. Well, at least Grandma was. I'm not sure what Mama was thinking. She was smiling, but there was a blank look in her eyes.

Carol and Beth ran up and gave me a big hug and wished me a happy birthday. Carol grabbed my hand and led me to a table that held the biggest birthday cake I had ever seen. There were all kinds of presents stacked on top of one another on a booth against the wall. The place was decorated with different colored balloons, streamers, and a big sign that read *HAPPY BIRTHDAY, ANGELA!* My whole class was there, along with several teachers and Mr. Dietz, the principal. Even some of the kids' parents came.

"Let's play some games." Carol grabbed my hand and pulled me toward the arcade room. Several kids followed. We played every game in there. We went into the next room and climbed through the tubes and then slid down the slide. "This is the best birthday ever!" I yelled to everyone.

"How were your other birthday parties?" Molly asked.

"This is my first one," I answered.

"What? You mean you have never had a birthday party?" Molly repeated.

I saw Mama sitting at one of the tables with Beth, Grandma, Mrs. Blake, and a few other mothers. A look of anger crosses her face. I knew right away I had made a colossal mistake, one that I would pay dearly for when I got home. If not then, I was sure it would be later.

I said a silent prayer and then continued to enjoy my birthday while it lasted. I was hoping Mama was having a good time so that maybe, just maybe, she would forget about what I'd said. The only thing I could do now was ... wait.

CHAPTER 23

PASTOR MOORE

The party went off without a hitch. Beth did a great job making sure everyone had a good time, especially me. We played a few birthday games, but for the most part, we played games in the arcade room. We went back into the party room and were served pizza, soda and chips. Beth called me to the front of the place. I noticed the candles on the cake were lit. Everyone joined in singing "Happy Birthday."

I closed my eyes and made a wish, and then blew out the candles. I wished for a better life. I was lost in thoughts of how fantastic this day has been when someone tapped me on the shoulder. I turned to find Mama standing there handing me a gift.

"This one is from me," she said, smiling proudly.

I opened it to find a beautiful watch. The band was dark pink with hearts and flowers. My very first wristwatch and I loved it.

"Here, let me help you with that," Mama said, taking it from my hand and fastening it on my wrist. "Your teacher told me you are doing very well in school so I thought a watch would make a perfect gift."

"Thank you. I love it." I gave her a big hug.

"Not so fast," she said, laughing. "There is more."

I removed the colored tissue paper and was thrilled to find a pair of earrings with a matching necklace and bracelet.

"My ears aren't pierced," I said, looking up at her.

"It's okay. I have made you an appointment to have that done right after the party as part of your birthday gift. That is, if you want them pierced," she added hesitantly.

"I do, but how did you know?" I asked, surprised.

"I am your mother, silly; any good mother knows what their daughter wants." She laughed while lightly tapping me on the nose.

I cringed at her touch. If she noticed, she never showed it. She handed me the next gift. I got a lot of cool things from everyone, but I loved Grandma's gift most of all. It was a gold chain with an angel. The angel's body was the color of my birthstone, which I thought made it the perfect birthday gift.

I felt sorry for Grandma. She looked pitiful sitting there with her arm in a cast, but she seemed to enjoy the attention she was getting from everyone. A few people even asked to sign it. She avoided the question when asked how she broke it. Carol saved the day by saying, "She fell, silly," as one nosy boy named Bobby just wouldn't stop asking. Grandma and I stared at each other, and the look in her eyes warned me not to say a word.

Everyone was having a wonderful time. Even Mama seemed to enjoy herself. I caught her smiling while talking to Beth and a few other ladies. At one point she also laughed out loud at something someone said. *Things just might turn around for the better once again.*

The party began to wind down, and people started leaving. I received lots of presents, and the cake and ice cream was delicious. A few of the mothers stayed to help with the cleanup. After everyone left, Carol and I went to the restroom, while Grandma, Mama, and Beth talked about whatever it is that adults discuss.

I stopped just outside the restroom door and told Carol I would wait for her. She shook her head, grabbed my arm and pulled me in the restroom with her. Once the door was shut and locked, she explained that she didn't need to use the bathroom, it was just an excuse to get me alone so she could find out what was going on between Mama and me. She noticed the dirty looks I had been receiving from her. I explained everything from the beginning and ended with Champ attacking her, how weird she was acting lately, and how I just knew I was in big trouble when we got home. I wasn't sure what she would do to me, but anything Mama did was never good, especially when she was mad.

"We have to think of something," Carol said. She began pacing back and forth. Then stopped and placed her hands on my shoulders.

"I have an idea," she said, wide-eyed.

"What?" I asked

"What if I come home with you and spend the night? You know she never does anything while I'm there, plus I can help you keep Champ busy and out of trouble. Then maybe when it's time for me to go home, she will have forgotten all about it. What do you think?"

"Yes! I think it's perfect," I said

"Go ahead and admit that I am a genius." She laughed.

"I will, but only if it works." I giggled

"Good, let's go ask our mothers," she said as she opened the door.

"No, Wait! I have to do something first, and I need your help." I didn't wait for a reply. I told her of the little country church I had seen behind the Pizza Place when we pulled in, and how I needed to get to it and say a quick prayer before going home.

She stared blankly at me. I wasn't sure if she thought I was crazy or if she was contemplating another plan. After a long pause, she finally said okay.

"That's it? You look at me like I am crazy, and then all you can say is *okay*?"

"My mind went blank; I do that sometimes," Carol said, and we both laughed.

We decided it was best if I snuck out the bathroom window while Carol stood watch. I emptied the trash can on the floor and turned it upside down, climbed on top, and hoisted myself the rest of the way out the window. No sooner had my feet touched the ground, I was off and running as fast as I could toward the church. I didn't stop until I was inside. I loved the look and feel of the place. It had a peacefulness about it that I couldn't explain if I tried.

I made my way down the aisle to the pulpit. I stopped briefly to look around and take in everything. There was nothing fancy about it. It was charming and spotless. I noticed the pews had cushions on the seats that were covered in red velvet; windows lined both sides; some were plain while every other one was beautiful stained glass. My primary focus was getting to the altar, saying a quick prayer, and then getting back before anyone realized I was gone.

I never noticed the minister when he walked in the door and stood there watching as I dropped to my knees and prayed aloud.

"Dear God. Hello, sir, it's me, Angela, but I wouldn't mind one bit if you want to call me *Angel*. That's what Grandma and everyone else calls me. Grandma says you know everything even before it happens, so I figure you already know what is going to happen when I get home. That's what I want to talk to you about. Well, Lord, it's like this. Mama has something wrong with her. She gets awfully mad for no reason and then takes it out on me. Grandma and my dog Champ try to protect me, so Mama makes sure to hit me when they aren't around. I need you to send someone who can help figure out what is wrong with her and why she is so mean. Lord, that woman is meaner than a rattlesnake. Sorry, God, but she is, and you already know that, so could you please send someone to help us? That is, if you don't mind. She needs salvation, she needs you, and I need you.

"Well, God, I have to go now before she finds out I left the Pizza Place. Oh, one more thing before I go. I want Carol to spend the night because Mama won't hurt me if she is there. Please let our moms say *yes*. In Jesus's name, I pray. Amen."

I stood to my feet and turned to walk away. That's when I saw the pastor sitting on the bench with his head bowed in prayer and tears streaming down his face.

"Hello," I said nervously. "Are you okay?"

He nodded, and without a word, he wiped tears from his eyes.

"I'm sorry for just walking in, but the door was open, and I needed to talk to God about something important."

"Don't you fret, young lady. The church doors are always open for anyone needing prayer. By the way, I'm Pastor Moore." He extended his hand. "I believe we met at the hospital."

"I remember. You're my grandma's friend."

"Yes, that's right, but I seem to have forgotten your name." He stooped down in front of me.

"My name is Angela, but everyone calls me Angel," I said as I shook his hand.

"It's nice to meet you again, Angel." He forced a smile. "If you are in trouble or need any help, I am here for you, and anything you tell me will be kept just between us."

"Yes, sir," I said, staring at the floor. After a long pause, it was he who broke the silence.

"Call me if you get into trouble or simply need to talk." He handed me a card with his name and phone number on it.

"Thank you; I have to go now. It was nice to meet you." I ran towards the door, and then stopped and turned, facing him. "Did you mean it when you said whatever I tell you will be kept between us?" I asked.

"Yes, I meant it," he answered. "Do you have something you want to tell me?"

"Yes, sir. There is something wrong with my mama. She stays upstairs in her room talking to herself, and she gets angry for no reason. When she gets really mad, her eyes change color, and it scares me."

"What do you mean they change color?" Pastor Moore asked.

"Well, sir, they turn black, and she acts crazy like she's a different person. The weird thing is that I'm the only one who notices it most of the time. Anyway, I have to get back to the Pizza Place before she realizes I'm gone, so I would appreciate it if you would pray for her, my Grandma, and also my dog Champ."

Pastor Moore stood with his hands crossed in front of him, quietly listening to every word I said. After I finished, he spoke and said he was leaving the church, but a new pastor would be taking over and I could talk to him about everything.

"No! I don't want to talk to anyone else, and you can't leave the church. You can't just walk away from something God has called you to do. At least, that is what my Grandma taught me. She also taught me that people don't come into your life by accident. Sometimes God places them there for a reason. Thanks anyway for the prayers." I turned and ran out the door and hurried back to find Carol was anxiously waiting for me.

"What took you so long?" she asked.

"Pastor Moore came in and talked to me. He is a very nice man."

"That's good," Carol said. "Now let's go ask our mothers if I can stay."

We hurried into the building, giddy with excitement, hoping and praying our mothers would say yes. Neither of them hesitated as they both nodded a quick yes. I threw my arms around Mama's neck, hugging her tight and whispered in her ear. "Thank you for making this the best birthday ever."

I am no dummy; I knew that would please Mama if I did that in front of Beth, and just maybe it would even change her mind about whatever she may have planned to do to me when we got home. I hugged and whispered the same thing to Beth. I knew she was the one who made all this possible. Without her and Carol, I wouldn't have even had a cake. I hated for the party to end, but on the bright side, they both agreed to let Carol spend the night, which made me feel safe, at least for tonight.

The ride home seemed faster than usual. Carol and I talked and laughed the whole way. Champ didn't meet us at the car like he used to, for the simple fact that he was tied up even while no one is home. I felt sorry for him. I know he didn't understand why I had to do things this way, but I had no other choice.

Carol and I raced to the backyard to untie Champ and then lead him into the woods. We walked around while he did his own thing. It felt terrific having my best friend staying overnight again. We stayed out as long as possible, but had to cut it short when we heard Mama calling for us to come in.

We reluctantly tied Champ back up and started walking toward the house. Mama met us at the door on her way out; she said she was going to town and would be back in a few hours. Grandma had gone to the ladies quilting club and wouldn't be home until much later. Carol and I were excited to have the house to ourselves. We promised Mama we would be good and not make a mess while she was gone.

She looked a little apprehensive about leaving, but after Carol convinced her we would not mess with anything, she took one last glance toward the staircase, and with a nervous smile, she turned and walked out.

"Okay, now that she is finally gone, let's do some exploring," Carol said as she started up the stairs.

"No!" I yelled. "You know we are not allowed up there, and if Mama found out, she would kill us both."

Carol snickered and stepped off the step. "Oh, Angel, don't be such a drama queen."

"Wow! I think that's the first time you have called me Angel," I said, hoping she didn't notice I'd changed the subject.

"Well, your Grandma calls you Angel, and you said yourself you like it much better, so I figured I would call you Angel from now on, if you don't mind." She smiled and trotted off toward the kitchen. I followed, relieved that she forgot about wanting to explore the upstairs. I also knew it was just a matter of time before she would eventually try it again. Just the thought of trying to keep an eye on Champ and now Carol made me feel drained.

CHAPTER 24

CURIOSITY

We grabbed a few cookies and a glass of milk, being extra careful not to spill any, and took it to my room. We watched a few of our favorite shows on television, turned on some music and danced and laughed until our sides hurt.

"I'll be right back; I need to go to the bathroom," I said. I paused at the door and looked back at Carol, who was sitting on the floor combing my doll's hair. "I will be right back, and then we can find something fun to do—or maybe play with Champ a little more before it gets too late."

"Okay," she replied without so much as looking up.

I ran to the bathroom as fast as I could. I admit I was a little nervous about leaving Carol alone for too long. I hurried and then washed my hands. I picked up the hairbrush and began running it through my hair, wondering why Carol's hair was always so much shinier and prettier than mine. I asked Grandma that question once, but she said she didn't think so, and that everyone had something about themselves they didn't particularly like.

Just as I was finishing up, I jumped upon hearing a shrill scream. It sounded like it was coming from upstairs. I knew it was Carol, and I was sure she had gone into Mama's room. I ran as fast and as hard as I could, praying the whole time that she hadn't. I met her as she reached the bottom of the stairs, shaking with fear.

"What's wrong?" I yelled, all the while hoping she wouldn't tell me

"It was horrible."

Just then the front door flew open, startling us both. We turned to find Mama standing in the doorway. I will never forget the look on her face when she saw us standing at the bottom of the stairs. She asked what all the screaming was about while continually glancing upstairs.

"W...w...we were playing," I stuttered.

"I saw a big hairy spider," Carol said. "It was the biggest, ugliest thing I have ever seen," she added, shivering.

"Where did you see it?" Mama asked, not taking her eyes off the room upstairs.

It was I who began shaking this time, fearing Carol's answer. I tried to think of something, but before I could get the words to come out, Carol pointed at the living room wall. "It was right there next to the window, and it was big and black and hairy."

"Well, hopefully it found its way out through a crack in the window frame," Mama said as she started up the staircase, stopping about halfway up. She kept her eyes focused on the door at the top of the stairs. She told us to stay out of trouble and to find something to do until dinner was ready.

"We'll play with Champ," I said as I headed for the door with Carol close behind me.

I ran, only stopping when we reached the edge of the woods.

"Whew, that was close," I said, breathing a sigh of relief

"You can say that again." Carol looked at the ground and sadness came upon her face.

"What's the matter?" I asked concerned.

After a few moments, she finally looked up and said, "Do you think I am going to go to hell for lying to your mom? I only made it to the top of the stairs, and that's when I saw an enormous hairy spider, so I ran back down."

Her question took me by surprise. I stared at the ground, searching for an answer. "No, Carol, I don't think you will. You did it for a good reason, and Grandma says if you feel bad afterward—"

"I feel awful," Carol interrupted.

"Well, that's good. Grandma says it's called conviction, and when you feel that, you can ask God to forgive you, and he will."

Her eyes lit up, and a huge smile spread across her face. "I will do that right now," she said as she folded her hands and said a silent prayer.

"I feel better already." She smiled.

"Great!" I said. "How about we go to my secret hiding place first and play with Champ later?" We ran around the house until we reached the hidden doorway. We slipped inside, quickly making our way to my hideout. The place was dustier than the last time I was there. So we began to clean. I got the bright idea to ask Mama if we could have her old broom, since she'd just bought a new one.

I told Carol to wait for me, as I hurried out. I ran around the house and upon the back porch. I listened at the kitchen door. Everything was silent, maybe a little too quiet, if you asked me. I found the old broom standing by the garbage can. I grabbed it and turned to leave, and almost ran into Mama. I had no idea how she came up behind me without my hearing her. But there she was, just the same. I let out a little squeal upon seeing her.

"Where do you think you are going?" she asked, glaring at me.

"I was coming to find you to ask if we can have your old broom." The words spilled easily from my lips.

"Oh, is that so?" she said sarcastically.

"Yes, ma'am." I met her gaze without blinking an eye.

"What are you going to use it for?" she asked. I figured she was just being nosy and once again trying to find a way to give me a rough time.

"I'm going to sweep Champ's house out and make it all nice and clean for him," I said with a smile. I knew I had to keep my word so I wouldn't be lying. I sure didn't want to feel any of that there conviction Carol felt. It looked like torture.

"Hey, where is everybody?" yelled Grandma, distracting Mama long enough for me to slip past her.

"Hi, Grandma! Goodbye, Grandma!" I yelled, running past her without so much as looking back. I quickly made my way to my secret place and helped Carol try to fix it up. We swept the dirt off the ground, revealing a hard, smooth dirt floor. We then spread the old blanket out like a throw rug. I found an old wooden crate and set it in the center for a coffee table. We also found some coloring pages and crayons I had left there during the summer, which we colored and then hung on random nails sticking through the wall. Stepping back to admire our handiwork, we looked at each other and smiled, pleased at how it turned out. I told Carol about the incident with Mama in the kitchen, and that I needed to sweep Champ's doghouse just in case she decided to check.

Champ was very excited to see us and didn't seem to mind when we cleaned and swept his home. I think he rather enjoyed a fresh, clean place. It even smelled better after I put new straw down for him. We laughed as Champ jumped and began rolling and digging at the straw and then tossing it everywhere with his nose. He loved it, and I loved watching him enjoy himself.

We were just finishing up when Grandma yelled for us to come in. After giving Champ a big hug, we raced to the house. I tossed the broom under the back porch before running up the steps. The house was filled with a delicious aroma. .

"Something smells good," Carol said.

"What smells so yummy?" I asked.

"Hot buttered popcorn," Grandma replied.

"Mmm, I love popcorn!"

"Me too," Carol said.

We sat at the table with Mama.

"How about taking it to the living room?" Mama suggested.

"Sounds good to me," I said.

Mama smiled and walked to the linen closet and pulled a blanket down off the shelf. She stretched it out on the floor, grabbed a couple pillows off the couch and tossed them on the blanket for Carol and me.

Grandma poured the popcorn in a bowl, carried it into the living room and set it on the coffee table. Mama put a movie in the DVD player. For the first time, there were no dirty looks or strange behavior. We had a lovely family night, and I enjoyed it.

Once the movie was over, Carol and I offered to help clean up, but Mama insisted on doing it herself. Therefore, we spent the rest of the evening in my room. Time seemed to fly. Before long, it was time for our baths and then bed. We were both exhausted and quickly drifted off to sleep.

CHAPTER 25

FLASHBACK

I awoke early the next morning to the sound of thunder rolling off in the distance. The sky was darker than usual due to the storm slowly moving in. *Oh, this is just great. If it rains, we'll have to stay inside all day.*

I sat up, still shaking from the horrible nightmare I'd had—it felt so real I couldn't stop thinking about it. I dreamt I was in the woods, running from something I couldn't see, yet I could feel its presence breathing down the back of my neck. I was screaming for Champ, but he never came. I was spinning and turning in every direction, trying to find him.

The trees seemed so dark and ominous with their outstretched branches like giant claws reaching out to grab me. I could feel the evil presence looming over me. I looked up to see eyes, but not just any eyes—it was Mama's eyes, even colder and darker than usual. I ran, trying to get away. I found my way out and was coming to an open area when I spotted something just beyond the trees where the field and woods met. My heart skipped a beat as I realized it was Champ. He was lying on his side, covered in what appeared to be blood.

"God, please don't let Champ die," I pleaded in a whispered prayer while running toward him as fast as I could. It was as though I was on a treadmill, running in place. I was slowly approaching him when thunder or something woke me.

I shivered at the thought of ever losing Champ, and repeated the same prayer from my dream silently to myself. A tear escaped my eye and made its way down my cheek. I wiped it away with the back of my hand as Carol began to stir. I didn't want her to see me crying over a stupid dream.

Too late, she noticed and asked what was wrong. I had just finished telling her my dream when I heard a knock on the bedroom door. It was Grandma, letting us know breakfast was ready. We raced to the kitchen, with Carol in the lead. The kitchen was empty except for the three of us. Mama was upstairs—which could only mean one thing—this was not going to be a good day. I shivered at the thought.

Grandma had my full attention upon announcing she had made chocolate chip pancakes for breakfast. I had never had them, so I was eager to try them. She placed two on my plate, then topped them off with maple syrup and butter. After one bite, I was hooked. The flavor combination exploded in my mouth. I told her that I wouldn't mind having them every morning. She smiled proudly, the way she always did when anyone complimented her cooking.

Carol seemed to enjoy them as much as I did.

We hurried and ate, and were just getting ready to go outside when Beth called to say she was on her way to pick up Carol. I hated to see her leave but knew it was best. Something terrible was about to happen, I could feel it in my bones. I wasn't sure what, but there was no doubt that it had everything to do with Mama. Even Grandma seemed more on edge today than usual. I thought she was going to have a heart attack when Champ got loose and jumped up on the back door wanting in. I hurried outside and tied him up.

Beth showed up at eleven a.m. sharp. Carol and I gave each other a quick hug before she raced out the door. I stood and watched as they drove out of sight. I closed the door and was staring toward the staircase as a strong feeling of dread came over me. I couldn't help but wonder what was so secretive about the upstairs that Mama seemed on edge all the time—as well as overly protective about it.

CHAPTER 26

CHAMP

I tried to keep myself preoccupied with other things for the rest of the day. I took Champ for a walk down the road. We turned around before reaching Old Man Sims' place and took our time walking back home. Champ seemed to have enjoyed the time away from home as much as I did. I had to call him several times when he would go racing off into the woods after a rabbit or squirrel, barking the whole time.

It was late when we got back. I tied Champ to his doghouse, which he despised. He whined as I walked away. I hated it, but knew it was for the best.

I walked through the front door, hoping Mama hadn't noticed the time—or that I had even been gone, for that matter. I stood staring up the stairs a few minutes before walking to the window and looking out making sure Champ was still tied up.

I felt a hand grip the back of my neck just before my face smashed against the window. Mama pressed me hard against it. The glass cracked and popped, threatening to break from the pressure. I just knew it was going to shatter, possibly cutting my throat.

Champ went crazy trying to break free, lunging harder and harder against the chain. I was hoping and praying he wouldn't get loose. I was unsure of what he would do if he ever got a hold of Mama—or if I'd be able to stop him.

She spun me around, yelling nonstop. I lost my balance and fell to the floor. She kicked me in the side, knocking the breath out of me. I lay there, fighting to breathe, while she stood over me, screaming. Her voice was becoming shrill as she raged about keeping Carol away from the staircase.

I managed to get up on my hands and knees, only to crumple back on the floor, fighting to catch my breath. Just then, the window above my head shattered. I closed my eyes to avoid getting shards of glass in them.

Mama let out a blood-curdling scream.

Champ had broken his chain. Part of it still dangled from his collar. He jumped through the window to protect me, and now had Mama by the arm, shaking and growling as they spun around and around. She was trying to shake him loose, and he was refusing to comply. The more she tried to pull away, the harder he shook his head. She was bleeding profusely from a big gash in her arm and screaming for me to get my dog. After catching my breath and forcing myself to my feet, I yelled at him in a half-hearted effort, "Champ! No! Stop!"

But it was no use. He refused to turn her loose.

I grabbed him by the collar and yelled again for him to stop.

He immediately let go, jumped up on me, and began licking my face. His face was covered in blood, Mama's blood, and he was in big trouble.

Mama ran to the bathroom to clean and bandage her wounds. In the meantime, I took Champ to the kitchen sink, wet a paper towel, and began cleaning him up as best I could.

"Oh, no. Champ, you have done it now," I whispered. "I better tie you back up and hope Mama doesn't do anything drastic."

She was upstairs, yelling and talking to herself.

Holding onto his collar, I walked him to the back door. Placing my hand on the knob, I started to turn it when I heard footsteps behind me. I turned to find Mama standing there with a gun in her hand, pointing it at Champ.

"No!" I shouted, stepping in front of him and tightening my grip on his collar.

"Move out of the way, Angela!" she demanded.

I had to think of something fast. I could feel my heart beating as though it were going to burst through my chest. My mind racing, I yelled, "Grandma, stop her!"

Williams

When Mama turned to find no one there, I opened the door and shoved Champ outside. I waved my arms and yelled for him to run. He must have sensed the urgency in my voice, because I had never seen him run so fast. I figured it was either that or the fact that Mama was screaming at the top of her lungs that I was in for it and she was going to kill that good-for-nothing dog.

Champ stopped and looked back; he kept looking toward the forest then back at me as though he were undecided on which direction to go.

Mama ran down the stairs with me not far behind her. She cussed and screamed, and threatened to shoot him if given half a chance. She stopped long enough to pick up a rock and throw it at him. He jumped as it bounced in front of him.

By then I had caught up with her, wrapped my arms and legs around hers and held on for dear life, begging and pleading all the while for her not to hurt Champ.

At first, she tried to continue walking with me attached to her leg. The more she struggled to move, the angrier she became until she'd had finally had enough. She bent down and began to pummel me with one hand while aiming the gun at Champ with the other. Finally, she punched me hard in the face over and over until I had no choice but to turn loose. I lay there on the ground and felt the all too familiar warmth of blood seeping from a gash somewhere on my head and running down my face as well as from my nose. The pain was excruciating; I could hardly move. As I lay there looking up at the sky, I whispered a little prayer asking God to protect

Champ. I had seen him running toward the woods with Mama not far behind. "I love you, Champ," I whispered.

Drained of all strength, my head dropped to the ground.

The night started closing in, and rain began to fall, making an eerie sound as it fell through the treetops. I strained to listen for any sign of Champ or Mama coming back. Too weak to move, all I could do was lie there with my eyes closed while the rain gently washed away the blood from my face. Just before losing consciousness, I heard a gunshot.

I awoke to find myself in my bed, dressed in my favorite pink nightgown with no sign of blood anywhere. *Maybe it was all a bad dream.* The pain shooting through my body reminded me otherwise.

Perhaps it was thunder I'd heard and not a gunshot.

I eased out of bed and slowly stood. The pain coursing through my body was almost unbearable. I walked hunched over, with my arms across my ribs, and made my way to the window. I pulled back the curtains, hoping to see Champ lying in his usual spot, waiting for me to sneak him into my room.

There was no sign of him. I looked toward his doghouse, praying he was chained to it. It stood empty instead. I quietly stood there peering into the darkness for what felt like hours, but there was no sign of him anywhere.

Tears flowed down my cheeks as I slumped to the floor, curling myself into a ball. I lay there and cried until I had nothing left. I sat up with knees drawn to my chest and sat there snubbing—as Mama always called it—from crying so hard and so much. She hated when I did that. I didn't care; I hated her. I hated everything about her. I hated how she treated Grandma, how she treated me, and especially how she treated Champ. God help me, I hated her.

I heard Grandma's words softly ringing in my ears. "No, child! Don't allow hatred to seep into your heart. Don't allow the evil things your mother has done consume you. You are better than that."

Come to think of it, where was Grandma? I hadn't seen her since she had left for her quilting club. Mama said she was spending a few days with one of the ladies, helping to organize everything for the fall festival. They always set up a bake sale and raffled off the quilt they worked on all summer. The proceeds were donated to one of the local charities. Even so, she should have been home by now.

My mind began to race. What if Mama killed her too? "No! You can't think that," I whispered aloud. Besides, I had overheard Mama on the phone with her when she called to say she would be away for a few days.

I erased the thought from my head. I had enough to worry about with Champ missing, plus I had no doubt my ribs were broken and possibly my nose as well. It was hurting and swollen so much I could hardly breathe. I didn't have time to worry about myself. I may have been injured, but at least I was still alive. I had to find Champ and make sure he was all right. That's all that mattered.

I spent the better part of the day devising a plan to get out of the house and search for Champ. No matter what I came up with, nothing seemed to work. Mama was always home, and I didn't want to think about what she would do if she caught me, especially if she knew why. I was sure if Champ were alive, he was now at the top of Mama's List of Enemies.

I lay down, exhausted and sore, and fell fast asleep. I had a restless night tossing and turning. The only good thing about it was that I saw Champ again in my dreams. We were running through the fields chasing butterflies and birds. We were having fun, and we were both happy.

I awoke at daybreak to a thumping sound coming from upstairs, which wasn't unusual. Mama was always making noises up there, banging on one thing or another and talking to herself. I lay there listening for a while, wondering what she could be doing. One thing I knew for sure was that she was hiding something. The more I thought about it, the more my curiosity grew, and I was determined to find out what it was.

My decision was final. I would wait until she went into town, then run upstairs and take a quick peek in her room. What harm could it do? I would step inside and make sure not to touch anything. *You can do this,* I told myself, all the while fighting off the sick feeling growing in the pit of my stomach.

I heard Mama outside my door fidgeting with the lock. I pulled the blankets over my head and rolled over on my side with my back toward the door. I listened as she entered the room and walked around the bed to the nightstand where she placed my breakfast tray, I figured she was trying to make up for what she did to me and possibly Champ, but she hadn't apologized for anything, nor would I accept an apology if she did.

This had become her morning routine. Only this time, someone was with her.

"No, I can't do this. Please don't make me do it," Mama begged.

"Shut up!" a male voice said. "You will do this or suffer the consequences."

"We have no use for a cowardly fool." This time it was a scratchy, yet high-pitched voice. I couldn't tell if it were a male or female. I wanted to pull the blankets down and take a peek but was too afraid of getting caught.

"Hush, the child is listening!" the deep male voice whispered.

"No! She's sleeping. I swear she is," Mama said in a low, panicked tone.

"No matter, she will join us soon," the scratchy, high-pitched voice said.

"Why her?" Mama whispered a little louder. "She is just an innocent little girl."

"She is almost of age. Her gift grows stronger, and we must destroy her before she learns of it," the deep male voice said angrily.

"What gift?" Mama asked. "What are you talking about?"

Everything grew quiet. I knew they were still there, so I lay as still as I possibly could. Finally, curiosity got the better of me. I eased the blankets up and peeked out from under them. There was no one else in the room, except for Mama. *So, where did the voices come from?* A chill ran down my spine when I realized they were coming from her. I slowly pulled the blanket back down and listened.

I heard footsteps walk across the room and out the door. Only this time, much to my surprise and relief, Mama forgot to lock it. The only problem with that was the hinges creaked whenever the door moved, and I wasn't sure if she'd left it unlocked to allow me to escape or as a trap.

The phone rang, I eased out of bed and pressed my ear against the door. Mama picked up on the third ring. "Yes, Mother, Angela is fine. She's in her room … Virginia? How long are you going to be gone? … Okay… yes, I will take the phone to Angela. Hold on a sec."

I panicked, ran and jumped back into bed. Excruciating pain shot through my ribs. I lay there, writhing in pain when Mama entered, phone in hand. "Angela, your grandma's on the phone and wishes to speak with you." She handed me the phone. I knew from the look on her face that I had better keep my mouth shut.

"Hello, Grandma."

"Hey, sweetie, are you all right?"

"Yes, I'm fine," I answered, trying to keep the quiver out of my voice that would give away the lie.

"I called to tell you that I am on my way to Virginia."

"Virginia?" I shouted.

"I'm sorry that I couldn't see you before I left, but my friend is very sick and her prognosis isn't good, so I had to leave right away."

"I hope your friend gets well soon."

"Honey, are you sure you're all right?"

"I just don't feel well today. I—"

Mama snatched the phone from my hand. "She has a stomach bug, Mother. She will feel much better tomorrow … Yes, I promise I will take her to the doctor if she isn't better by then. Have a safe trip and hurry home." She hung up the phone and left the room.

I lay there feeling abandoned and scared. I softly sobbed into my pillow.

When Mama came back into my room, I pretended to be sleeping. She walked over and closed the window. "Angela, are you awake?" she whispered.

I lay still, hoping she would leave.

"I know you're awake," she said. "Well, just so you know, don't bother trying to sneak out the window. I have alarms on all of them. If you so much as touch one, I will know."

My heart sank. *What am I going to do now?*

So, there I was back to square one, still trapped in my room, only this felt much worse. I hated the thought of knowing I had a way out but couldn't take it out of fear. I needed to talk to Grandma and find out what she thought I should do, but she had to go to Virginia to take care of a sick friend, and she didn't know when she would be home.

CHAPTER 27

THE MEETING

Days turned into weeks. I missed Grandma dearly. The thought of her coming home was the one thing I had left to look forward to. I stopped counting on day five, so I didn't know how long it had been. I stood staring out the window at the spot I last saw Champ. Tears began to well and slowly started to make their way down my cheeks. I quickly wiped them away with the back of my hand. I could have kicked myself for not doing more to save him.

Deep down, I knew there was nothing more I could have done. I could hardly think straight, let alone get up, due to the severe beating I withstood. I had to keep reminding myself of that. I couldn't allow guilt to set in. Like Grandma always says, the feeling of guilt leads to depression. Say a prayer and then reason things out. God always gives us a way out, so look for the window of opportunity and take it.

Suddenly, it dawned on me. The window. The day Grandma left, Mama had opened and closed the window. If there was an alarm on it, why didn't it go off? I had a way out all along. I could climb out the window. Why hadn't I thought of this before? But then again, pain, grieving, and fear were all I could think about.

I would test it. If an alarm went off, I'd tell Mama I wanted some fresh air and forgot. I unlocked the window, took a deep breath, and slowly slid it open. There were no ringing or buzzing sounds whatsoever. *Oh, my gosh, she lied. There are no alarms.*

I could hardly contain my excitement. Not only was I going to get out of the house after God only knew how long, but I was also going to get a chance to search for Champ. I finally saw a light at the end of the tunnel for the first time in days.

The day seemed to pass more slowly than usual. I knew it was due to the anticipation of finally getting out and searching for Champ. A sick feeling came over me when I realized I would now be searching for Champ's body. I needed to find him and give him a proper burial. He deserved that much.

I busied myself with cleaning and homework. While cleaning, I happened upon a black, long-sleeved shirt I had stuffed under the dresser. Champ was the last one who wore it. I tied it around his neck, pretending it was a cape and he was a superhero. I hid it there months ago, and I was lucky Mama hadn't found it. I cringed at the thought of what would've happened if she had.

This shirt was perfect. All I needed to do now was find the black jeans Carol had given me. I looked in the closet and saw them hanging in the back corner. When the time was right, I would slip them on and sneak out. I was hoping by dressing all in black, no one could see me in the dark, especially in the woods. I figured no one would be out that late at night other than wild animals, but with Champ's scent still on the shirt, maybe it would deter any animals from coming near me. At least, that was what I was hoping.

The evening seemed to drag by, but I didn't mind much. I busied myself working out the details of my plan. My timing had to be perfect to avoid getting caught. With Mama in and out of the house so much, I would take the opportunity to sneak out of my room, call Carol, and fill her in on everything, including the details of my plan. I hated involving her, but I didn't have much choice. I needed her help for this to work.

I lay down on the bed and let out a sigh of relief, pleased with myself for coming up with what I believed to be the perfect plan. Now all I had to do was to wait.

I lay there daydreaming when the door creaked open. I sat straight up in bed, unable to move as I watched Mama walk in. She looked tired, worn, and much older than she was.

"Mama, are you all right?" I asked.

"No, Angel, I'm not," she replied. *Angel.* She never called me *Angel.*

"Listen to me," she continued. "I need you to stay as far away from me as possible, at least until I can figure out what to do. Do you understand?" she asked, almost in a panic.

"Yes, ma'am," I answered.

"I am going to call Beth and see if she will take you in for a little while. It's too dangerous for you to be here." She grabbed her stomach, doubled over, and screamed.

I jumped off the bed and took a step toward her. She threw her hand out and yelled for me to stop and not come any closer. She then hurried into the living room, picked up the phone and dialed a number I assumed was Beth's. Just as she placed the phone to her ear, she let out a loud scream, put her hands over her ears, and dropped the receiver. She ran back upstairs to her room, slamming the door behind her.

I stood dumbfounded—and scared. I stepped back into my room, closed the door, and said a prayer for both of us. I missed Grandma more than ever and could hardly wait for her to come home. It seemed like she had been gone for years instead of—what was it now, two, or three weeks? It had been so long, I'd lost track. I wondered how she was going to react to the news about Champ, and also the fact that Mama had completely lost it.

My door still creaked, which could be a problem for me should I try to sneak out to call Carol. I had to think of something. I searched the top shelf of my closet until I found Grandma's can of sewing machine oil. She had forgotten it in my room when she was teaching me to sew. "Yes! Thank you,

Grandma." I squirted some on the door hinges to keep it from creaking. It would make it easier to sneak out, but I also knew it would make it harder to hear if anyone else came in. It was a chance I had to take.

Several days went by without incident; in the meantime, I thought I would go crazy from boredom. On a good note, Grandma would be coming home soon, and I was so excited I could hardly wait. What would be even better is if Champ were here with me to greet her. I couldn't delay sneaking out to look for him any longer—even though I was afraid of what I might find.

I slid the little flashlight in my jeans pocket, slipped on my shoes, and said a prayer. I opened the window as quietly as possible, pushing one leg out and then the other. I gently dropped to the ground. "I made it," I whispered.

Now for the hard part—finding Champ's body and then climbing back in without getting caught. And then the thought crossed my mind, what am I going to do should I see him alive and well? I can't bring him home with me; Mama would kill us both for sure. Oh, well, I would figure that out when the time came.

I kept as close to the house as I possibly could. I stood still for a moment, listening. All was quiet.

The night was pitch black. The moon and stars refused to shine. It was as though God had darkened them just for me. I made it to the back of the house and stared into the darkened field that lay before me. It was now or never, I thought as I ran toward the area where I'd last seen Champ. I stopped when I made it to the edge where the field and woods met. I turned and looked back towards the house. It appeared dark and ominous. It reminded me of one of the haunted houses in the movies Mama always watched.

"No turning back now," I whispered. My heart pounded in my chest as I entered the woods. It was darker than I ever imagined. It was so dark, I couldn't see my hand in front of my face. Reaching into my pocket, I pulled out the flashlight, but decided against turning it on for fear of Mama seeing it and coming after me. I didn't want to think about what she may do if she knew I was no longer locked in my room.

I slowly made my way deeper and deeper into the woods, knowing all the while that I could get lost if I wasn't careful. I figured if I walked a straight line, I could find my way back by following the same straight path. At least, that was the plan. Dry leaves and twigs popped and cracked with every step. The sounds seemed to echo into the night.

When I thought I was out of view, I slid my hand into my pocket and pulled out the flashlight. I was just about to turn it on when I heard footsteps coming toward me. I froze in my tracks. I was sure Mama had found me. I said a silent prayer as I stood there hiding behind a tree, peering into the darkness and trying to figure out from which direction the noise had come from. Whatever or whoever it was had also stopped walking.

What if it wasn't Mama at all, but a huge bear? I think I would rather face a bear than Mama.

Better yet, what if it were Champ coming to find me? "Champ, is that you, boy?" I whispered. Everything became eerily quiet, which only added to the spookiness of being alone in the woods at night.

I slowly pressed the button on the side of the light and shined it around the tree—right into a wrinkled old face.

Just as I was about to scream, a large hand clamped over my mouth. "Shush, girl, and turn off that light," came a deep male voice. "Now, I'm going to remove my hand if you promise not to scream. Do you promise?"

I nodded as I flipped off the light. I no longer needed it, since the moon decided to show its face after all, and was peeking through the treetops giving off enough light to see the dark figure of the man who stood before me.

"Who are you?" I asked, my voice filled with fear.

"I'm Jud Sims, your neighbor from down the road," he replied. "What in the heck are you doing wandering these woods at night, young lady?"

"I was looking for my dog."

"Looking for your dog, huh?" He stood there rubbing the stubble on his chin as if pondering what to say next.

"Please don't tell Mama," I begged.

"Now don't you fret, child. I know she's your mama and all, but that woman just ain't right in the head. As a matter of fact, she's downright loony toons."

"I know she is, and that's why I have to sneak upstairs as soon as possible. I just have to find out what she has hidden there."

"Well, kiddo." Mr. Sims scratched his head. "I'm not sure if that's a good idea."

What if Champ is there and needs my help? I thought.

He must've read my mind. He placed his hand on my shoulder, giving it a little squeeze.

"I was out hunting a while back. It grew dark before I made it back to my truck, parked just over the hill there." He pointed in the same direction I had been walking. "I heard a dog barking, so I went to see what all the fuss was about. I saw your mama in the field, but couldn't make out what was going on. That's when I heard gunshots. As a matter of fact, one of the bullets whizzed past my head. I saw her heading in my direction. That's when I figured it was time for me to skedaddle."

"She was shooting at Champ," I said.

"Why?"

"Mama beat me within an inch of my life, and Champ tried to protect me," I answered.

"Well, I don't like to meddle in other people's business, but I figured something like that was going on. After that, I made it a point to keep an eye and ear out for you every night."

"So you're like my guardian angel," I said. "Now I have three guardian angels—Grandma, you, and Champ." My voice trailed off as it dawned on me that Champ was no longer one of them.

We stood there in silence, our heads bowed in sorrow. Tears pooled in my eyes and slowly trickled down my cheeks. I broke the silence. "I love and miss Champ so much it hurts,"

"I'm sure he loves and misses you even more," Mr. Sims said.

"How do you know that?" I asked.

"Well, kiddo, if he didn't, he wouldn't have been so protective."

"He still tried his best to protect you even with a crazy woman shooting at him."

"You couldn't have chosen a better name for him," Mr. Sims said, smiling.

"I agree. There will never be another quite like him. Thank you for talking with me, Old Man Sss . . . uh, I mean, Mr. Sims, but I guess I better head back home now before Mama realizes I'm gone."

"Listen, child; there is something you must know," he said, but before he could finish, something caught his attention.

I turned to see what it was, only to realize I hadn't walked as far as I'd thought. I could see the house, and the upstairs light was now on, which meant one of two things. Either Mama had gotten up to go to the bathroom, or she'd found out I was gone.

We stood, watching and waiting. I prayed silently to myself that she had just gone the bathroom. Finally, after several nerve-racking moments, the light went back off.

"Welp, it looks like she has gone back to bed," Mr. Sims said. "I figure you best wait a while before heading back. You know, give her a chance to fall asleep." He gently nudged me. "You don't need to go and get yourself caught."

"Yeah, I guess you're right." I said.

We sat silently listening to the sounds of the night. An owl hooted from a nearby tree. I noticed things sounded much different in the daytime. It seemed as though all the bugs, frogs, crickets and an occasional coyote decided to sing their song at once. After a few moments, I interrupted their symphony. "Mr. Sims, did you know my dad?" I asked.

"Yes, child, I sure did. As a matter of fact, I was his boss. He worked for me in the coal mines."

"What was he like?

"He was a good man and a good friend. You look like him, you know."

"Really?" He had my full attention.

We sat and talked a while longer. I loved hearing all the funny stories Mr. Sims told me about my dad. Things I never knew because Mama didn't talk about him and hated if I asked questions. My favorite story was when Daddy took me to the company barbeque and proudly showed me off to all his friends and co-workers.

"Your daddy would toss you in the air and play silly games like peek-a-boo, airplane—anything to make you laugh—and then he would hug you tight and tell you how much he loved you," Mr. Sims said. "When your daddy and mama got the news of her pregnancy, they were the happiest couple on earth. They were so ecstatic upon your arrival that he passed out cigars to everyone at work and even strangers on the street showing off your picture to everyone he met."

We sat in silence as I took it all in.

"Well, child, I guess you best be getting back. I figure your mama is fast asleep by now," Mr. Sims said. I could tell he was a little worried, even though he tried to hide it.

He walked me out of the woods, stopping at the edge of the field, and stood for a moment as if pondering on something. After a long pause, he finally spoke, "I promise I will continue to be here in this very spot every night, watching and listening for you come, rain or shine."

"Thank you so much," I said and hugged him.

I turned to leave, but Mr. Sims stopped me once again by placing a gentle hand on my shoulder. "Listen to me, child. When you are safe and sound back in your room, shine your flashlight out the window and click it on and off once to let me know that everything is all right. Should at any time things get out of hand, I want you to shine it out the window and click it on and off twice, and I will be there in a heartbeat."

I promised him I would. We said our goodbyes, and I reluctantly headed back home.

I didn't waste any time making my way through the open field toward the house. The closer I got to the house the more massive and uninviting it appeared. I felt as though it held more dark secrets within its very walls than anyone could ever imagine. I tried to think of happier times, but at that moment, as hard as I tried, I just couldn't think of any. I made it to the back corner of the house, which felt more like a prison than it ever did a home.

Just as before, I stayed close to the house until I made it to my bedroom window. That's when I realized I had a huge problem. My window was too high off the ground for me to climb back in. I knew that I couldn't place something in front of it to stand on because once inside I had no way of moving it to keep Mama from finding out I had left my room. Panic set in. I pressed my back against the house and slid down to my usual sitting position with my knees drawn to my chest and my head down. *What am I going to do now?*

I was just about to give up hope of getting back in through the window when I heard a familiar voice whisper, "Here, let me help you."

I looked up to see Mr. Sims standing over me. He kept looking around, making sure the coast was clear. "Hurry, Angel, before your mother catches us both."

I scrambled to my feet, and he lifted me up to the window. Once inside, I ran to my bedroom door. I slowly cracked it open, then peered into the darkened living room and listened. Everything was still and quiet. After a few moments, I eased the door shut and then ran back to the window to assure Mr. Sims that everything was fine. He waved goodbye, and then quickly made his way back across the field and disappeared into the woods.

I changed into my pajamas and then crawled into bed, pulling the blankets over my head. I lay there thinking of everything Mr. Sims and I talked about, especially my daddy. Mr. Sims' words played over and over in my mind. "Your father was a good man whom everyone loved, and he loved you more than life itself." I knew nothing about him until that night. Oh, how I longed to have him here with me now. I tried imagining what he looked like and how different life would've been with him here.

I knew one thing for sure; he would never have allowed Mama to raise a hand to me—nor anyone, for that matter. I smiled at the thought, and then rolled over to my side, slid the blankets down over my shoulders and fell fast asleep.

CHAPTER 28

TENDER MOMENT

I awoke to find Mama sitting in a chair next to my bed, staring at me. I jumped upon seeing her. She stood and moved around to the other side of the bed. I thought she was going to leave, but she sat down next to me, bent over and gently kissed my forehead.

"Mama, is something wrong?" I asked nervously.

"Yes, baby girl, something is terribly wrong," she answered in a depressed tone.

Baby girl? Did I hear her right? She had never called me that before.

We sat in awkward silence for several minutes. I stared out the window and she at the floor.

When she raised her head to speak, I noticed tears streaming down her face. "Angel, I want you to know I love you more than life itself. I am sorry for all the hell I put you through. I did it all to save your life. You may not understand any of it now, but one day you will, and I hope you can forgive me. I haven't been myself since your daddy died, and I'm not sure how I can fix things between us. No matter what happens, always remember that I love you with all my heart." She grabbed my arms and pulled me to her and held me for the longest time, sobbing uncontrollably.

She then stood, wiped the tears from her face, and left the room, leaving me more confused than ever. I put my hands together and said a little prayer for her, asking God to fix whatever the problem was and to give me the mother that I longed for, this one, the tender loving woman who just walked out.

The next day started out gloomy. I met Mama as I was coming out of the bathroom. I froze.

"Angela, if you want breakfast, there is cereal in the kitchen." Mama was on edge about something. She hurried through the house mumbling to herself, shoving stuff in a clear plastic bag. I could see that one of the items was a book on witchcraft.

"I'll get rid of you once and for all," she said and placed a few more books in the bag.

I returned to my bedroom, closed the door, and pressed my ear against it.

The phone rang. Mama picked up the receiver. "Hello?" Her voice quivered nervously. "Oh, no, no, I am fine, just busy at the moment … Yes, Angela's fine… What?.. Today?... What time?... No, I'm not upset you're coming home, it's just that it will take me two hours to get there, I am in the middle of something and have a few errands to run first … Okay, I will pick you up this evening. Bye."

I was pretty sure it was Grandma, because Mama sounded aggravated. She hung up, grabbed her keys, yelled to me that she would be home later, and then rushed out the front door. I heard the car start up and then head down the driveway. I ran to the window in time to watch her drive out of sight.

A mixture of excitement as well as fear washed over me. I nervously walked across the bedroom to the door and listened. Upon feeling certain no one else was there, I slowly twisted the doorknob, being extra careful that it didn't click, and ever so gently opened the door. The oil on the hinges worked like a charm.

I peeked into the living room, making sure the coast was clear, even though I had watched Mama drive down the road. I was still being extra careful. .. I tiptoed to the phone and called Carol.

Thankfully, she answered on the first ring.

"Carol, it's me, Angel."

"Oh, my goodness, it's so good to hear your voice. I've missed you so much. How are you? I've been worried sick about you."

"Breathe, Carol," I said, laughing. "It's good to hear your voice as well. Listen, I don't have much time. Mama left, and I'm not sure how long she will be gone. I wanted to let you know that I'm going to check out her room the first chance I get. I have to know what she's hiding up there. And it looks like tonight may be my only opportunity. I overheard her say something about a long trip this evening. I think she's picking up Grandma."

"What! Are you crazy? You know what will happen if she catches you," Carol said quietly.

"I know, but I have to at least try. I need to find out what she is hiding."

"Just don't get yourself beat to a bloody pulp." She paused, then said in a low voice. "Angel, I have something to tell you, but you're not going to like it."

"I have so much to tell you to. You're not going to believe everything that has happened since we last talked."

"All right, you go first," she said.

I updated her on everything that happened up to this point, including the night that I ran into Mr. Sims. Well, I should say almost everything, because I left out the part about the voices, I overheard Mama talking to in my room. I knew Carol would flip out and tell her mom, who would call the police. And then I would never find out what she was hiding because, like always, Mama would convince them we were lying. I don't even want to think about the punishment that would ensue after that. When I had finished speaking, there was dead silence, and I began to wonder if we had gotten disconnected.

"Are you there?" I asked.

"Yes, I am still here. I'm just trying to process everything."

"What were you going to tell me?" I asked.

"Promise you won't get mad?" she asked.

"I promise."

"Well . . . ." She paused. From the sound of her voice, I knew it couldn't be good. "When I didn't hear from you for so long, I was afraid of what might have happened and told my mother about everything. She said she already suspected it, but since she never witnessed anything nor saw any unexplained bruises, she had no way of knowing."

We both grew quiet.

This time it was she who broke the silence. "Are you mad?"

"No, I'm not mad. As a matter of fact, I'm happy that you told her. At least she can attest to the fact that my grandmother isn't lying, nor is she crazy. Mama is being nice and loving right now, so you know what that means."

"Yes, the calm before the storm. Angel, please don't go up there. Your mom is going to lose it, and I hate to think of how bad things could get if she finds out you were in her room."

"You're right. It's not a good idea," I said, trying to calm her, yet not changing my mind.

I knew she fell for it when she breathed a sigh of relief.

"I have to go, but I will call you later," I said, and quickly hung up before she had a chance to respond.

CHAPTER 29

UPSTAIRS

I checked the time. It was four o'clock when Mama pulled into the driveway—later than I thought. Which meant she would be leaving again soon to pick up Grandma.

She entered my room, looking as though she hadn't slept in days, and asked if I were hungry.

I was famished. I hadn't eaten anything since yesterday, and, according to her, neither had she. She told me to come to the kitchen and she would make us both a sandwich. I reluctantly followed her and took my seat at the far end of the table. Without a word, she opened the fridge and took out everything needed to make our dinner.

"Mama, are you all right?" I asked.

"No, baby, I'm not," she replied.

"Do you want me to say a prayer for you?" I asked. "Grandma says prayer works if you only have faith and believe."

"Pray if you like, but I'm not sure God will help me now with all the things I've done."

"Mama, God will forgive you, but you have to first forgive yourself."

"I can't. I just can't." She placed her hands over her face and began to sob.

I got up from the table and walked to the counter to stand beside her. She continued to cry, and my heart broke for her. I placed my hand on her shoulder to comfort her. She turned to me and hugged me tight.

"I love you, Mama, and I forgive you for everything," I whispered in her ear.

She sank to the floor and cried uncontrollably, tears flooding her face. I stooped beside her and held her to me; she laid her head on my chest and we both cried until there were no tears left.

I stood, pulled a few tissues from the box on the counter and handed them to her.

"Thank you, baby." She wiped her face and nose as she got up off the floor, sniffling the whole time. "Thank you for forgiving me when I can't even forgive myself. I'll have to work on that, because things have got to change, starting tonight as soon as I get back with your Grandma."

Without another word, we sat in silence at the table and ate our dinner. After we finished, Mama checked the time, and asked if I would like to go with her. I told her I would clean up while she was gone and also freshen up Grandma's room.

"I think your Grandma would like that," she said.

She grabbed her purse and I walked her to the door. She hugged me and then waved goodbye as she drove off.

Several hours passed. I cleaned the kitchen and finished Grandma's room and lay down on her bed. I was just starting to doze off when a loud noise woke me. I opened my eyes and noticed that it was already dark out. I listened, but didn't hear a sound. I looked out the window in time to see a raccoon had knocked over the trash can and was scurrying off with its prize.

Now was my chance. I retrieved a small flashlight from the nightstand drawer and slid it in my pocket. I rushed from the room, and then paused for a brief second in the living room. I was nervous, yet excited at the same time. Deep down, I was hoping to find Champ alive and well, locked in a closet or somewhere up there. I knew the chances of that were slim to none. Besides, he would be barking his head off, but I had to know for sure.

I stood at the foot of the stairs, trying to get up the nerve to proceed. "Okay, Angel, get a grip. Just get this over with." I ascended the stairs and noticed they creaked with each step I took. Everything sounded loud and seemed to echo throughout the house. I wondered why I never noticed it when Mama descended the staircase.

I brushed it off as nerves. I stopped halfway and almost changed my mind, but the thought of possibly never having another chance to find out what the big secret was outweighed my fear.

I decided it was best to run up the last few steps. Upon reaching the top, I was surprised to see how big the upstairs was. I knew about Mama's room, but didn't know there were other rooms as well—three, to be exact. I hurried to the end of the hallway and started with the last door on the right. I turned the knob and cracked open the door. I then slid my hand in along the wall, searching for a light switch, and flipped on the lights. It was empty. The other room was used for storage, and the third and closest one to Mama's room was a small bathroom. I was relieved to know that there was nothing scary about the second floor after all—at least not that I'd found so far. Now, it was time to investigate Mama's room.

Gently placing my hand on the knob, I opened the door. I had no problem finding a light switch. I pushed the door open to find a huge, well-decorated room. The bed stood against the far wall on the left next to a window. A nightstand on each side of the bed held family photos of Grandma and Grandpa and, I assume, the child was my mother. The photo that caught my attention was the one of a man, woman and a baby standing under a large maple tree. Upon closer inspection I recognized the lady was my mother. She was as thin as she is now, only more beautiful. She wore a yellow summer dress which showed off her tan, and she held a baby girl in her arms. I knew the baby had to be me, dressed in an adorable pink and white dress with a matching ribbon in my hair. If that was Mama and me, then that meant the man must be my father. He was very handsome, with his short black hair neatly combed to one side, bright blue eyes and gorgeous smile. He was dressed in a black polo shirt and blue jeans. My guess would be that the photo was taken at one of the company picnics that Mr. Sims told me about.

On the floor to the left of the bed was a huge pentagram. A Ouija board lay in the center, unlit candles were placed on each point of the star, and a shrine to Daddy was behind it on a stand against the wall. A photo of him stood in the middle. It was surrounded by candles. A book lay open on the corner of the table to a page that read *How to Communicate with the Dead*. I shivered at the thought. I walked back to the nightstand and tried to focus on our family photo. Mama and Daddy looked so happy.

I began to daydream about that day and what it must have been like to have both a loving father and a mother, the three of us living together as a family, in a happy, safe and secure home. An overwhelming sadness flooded my soul. I grieved the loss of the father I couldn't remember as well as my beloved dog. *I'm sure Daddy would have loved you, Champ.* I slumped to the floor and sobbed long and hard until there were no tears left. I stood and retrieved a tissue from the box on the nightstand. I have no idea how much time had passed, I was so lost in thought. I realized I was no longer alone in the room when I heard the floorboard creak behind me.

I turned around to find Mama standing there. She could clearly see I had been crying, and for a split second I thought I saw a loving-tenderness in her eyes, which quickly turned cold and dead. She glared at me. Without a word, she lunged at me. I moved just in time. I ran to the window, planning on jumping out, but soon realized it was too high. As I started toward the door, I heard something smash against the wall and shatter into a thousand pieces. The lights began to flicker, then went out completely, leaving the room pitch black.

I was extra careful not to make a sound as I crossed to the far side of the room. I stepped backward into the empty corner, letting the shadows fold around me like a blanket.

Around me, the old house creaked and moaned as we both waited. I could barely see her black figure in the darkness as she made her way to the window. She jerked the curtains open, letting the moonlight spill into the room. Thank God the clouds blocked out most of the moon, causing it to give off an eerie dimness that only made the room appear even creepier.

I watched in horror as she dropped to her knees and began to crawl around the room like a wild animal looking for its prey. She looked under the bed and behind stuff.

"Come on out, Angela. Mama wants to play," she hissed in a voice that sounded inhuman. "Come out, sweetie. I have your dog, and I will take you to him if you just show yourself," she said, softening her tone.

Champ! I thought. I took a step forward, just inches away from the soft light that poured through the window; my pale skin glowed like white marble, threatening to expose my hiding spot.

"I said get out here, you good-for-nothing little brat!" she shrieked. "I am going to cut you into little pieces and bury you with that good-for-nothing dog."

I quietly stepped back into the darkened corner, the shadows sliding about my body, hugging me tight like an invisible protector. Tears pooled in my eyes and spilled down my cheeks. I knew then my beloved Champ was never coming back.

"Guess what, Angela?" she continued. "Your precious piece of crap dog lay there that night in a pool of blood, still trying to crawl to you, thinking he could protect his poor little Angela. His whining got on my nerves, so I walked up to him, looked into his big sad brown eyes, and put a bullet in his brain." She let out an evil, sadistic laugh.

Anger and hatred coursed through my veins like a raging fire; threatening to burn everything in its path. She stood with her back toward me, cursing under her breath.

I saw my chance. I rushed up behind her, shoving her with all my might. She fell forward, hitting the edge of the mattress and then bouncing face down onto the floor. I ran around to the other side of the bed. Panic set in, and my mind went blank. I thought about crawling under the bed, hoping she didn't see me; but just as I bent down, the entire bed rose in the air as though attached to invisible ropes and shot across the room, hitting the wall behind me.

Williams

I didn't have time to consider what my next move was going to be or how she had the strength to do that. I stood, staring wide-eyed, with no place to run. I have no idea where she disappeared to nor what came over me, but I stood my ground. I'd had enough. Enough of the abuse, enough of her nasty name calling, and enough of her evil, glaring eyes and annoying laughter. I decided to treat her the same way she treated me.

I stood with my feet shoulder width apart as I planted myself in the middle of the room, peering into the darkness, unsure if she was even there. Yet, I was prepared, come what may.

"Come out and show yourself, Mother!" I shouted. "Or are you too scared?" I chided.

From the darkness came a hissing sound, which soon turned into a small growl as she stepped forward and now stood right in front of me, smiling and twisting her head from side to side, her face becoming distorted while wearing that all-too-familiar evil grin. She never once took her eyes off me.

I stood there looking her dead in the eyes, gritted my teeth, and boldly said, "Show yourself!"

The look on her face was pure shock and horror. She dropped to her knees and screamed, "No!"

I knew then I must be onto something, and so I shouted once more, "Show yourself now, coward!"

She fell forward and was now on all fours, a low guttural growl coming from deep within her. She screamed as her whole body began to shake, twist and writhe on the floor.

A mixture of fear and power washed over me. I boldly stood over her, smiling, no longer feeling like the victim for once. I loved the feeling of this new-found power and control.

That feeling was short lived. A black figure rose up out of her back. It opened its huge black wings, which stretched from one side of the room to the other. This thing was massive. It must have had at least a twelve-foot wingspan. It tilted its head back and let out the most godawful growl that shook me to the core. It looked down at me with its charred, black face. It appeared as though it had been burned in a fire. It grinned, showing its sharp jagged teeth, and ran its tongue over them as it glared down at me with the same evil, black eyes I had seen in Mama.

"You dare challenge me, little girl?" it demanded in a voice so deep it resonated through every fiber of my being.

Fear cut through me like a knife. I thought I knew fear when dealing with Mama, but standing there looking into the face of pure evil brought fear to a whole new level. I stood frozen. Unable to speak and unable to move, I sure couldn't run. It were as though an invisible force held me in place.

I tried to scream, but couldn't.

It just stood there glaring at me it was as though it were staring into my very soul, draining me of all energy and replacing it with the same hatred and anger I felt coming from it. Evil was now trying to consume me like a fire burning deep within.

I dropped to my knees as the very life was being sucked out of me. I felt there was no way out and everything started going dark. "God help me," I managed to whisper faintly just before collapsing face down on the floor.

Suddenly, the entire room lit up. At first, I thought the electricity had been restored, but this light was different. It was brighter than anything I had ever seen. I placed my hand in front of my face. It took a few minutes for my eyes to adjust to the light. When they finally did, what I saw shocked me be beyond belief. There stood the beautiful woman from my dreams. She was dressed in a long, flowing white gown, only this time she had an incredible pair of wings that shined like the sun with gold specks glistening throughout. Her dress shimmered and flowed like pure white smoke. I was in such awe, I couldn't take my eyes off her.

I rubbed my eyes, unsure of what I was seeing. Could I be dreaming, or possibly hallucinating? I looked and saw my lifeless body lying in a heap on the floor. "Am I dead?" I asked, although I didn't speak.

She looked right at me and spoke even though her mouth wasn't moving. "No, child, you're not dead, and this isn't a dream." Her voice was soft and gentle, unlike any I had ever heard or imagined. She was reading my mind and I hers.

"Are you my guardian angel?"

"Yes, I am, little one, and I have a message for you from God. He wants you to know that you have the power within you. You have been chosen to do God's work, and He wants you to know He will be with you always. Fear not. Remember the biblical things your grandmother taught you. You have the scriptures written on the tablets of your heart. Stay focused, have faith in God, and He will see you through this."

CHAPTER 30

THE BATTLE

I opened my eyes to find myself lying on the floor. I slowly raised my head and looked around the room to see where Mama was. The room remained dark except for the moonlight shining brightly through the window. I lay there, trying to assess the situation and figure out my next move. I would be lying if I said I wasn't afraid—I was scared to death. I had never seen anything like this. I sat up and looked around, trying to catch a glimpse of where this thing was hiding.

A movement in the far corner caught my attention. The candle went out, leaving me in total darkness. The clouds moved, allowing the moon to give off just enough light so I could see this thing crawling slowly toward me. It was blacker than the night and was slithering on the floor like a snake getting ready to attack its prey. The only thing that came to mind at that point was to get out, to run fast, and get as far away from it as I could.

I leaped to my feet, backed against the wall and began feeling behind me, all the while keeping my eyes on the black heap crawling across the floor, growling and coming for me. It stopped, reared its head back, and let out a high-pitched scream.

Just then my hand landed on the doorknob. I jerked the door open and ran with all my might down the stairs, through the kitchen, and out the back door. I had no idea where I was going. I just knew I had to hide, and there was no time to run toward the woods or even down the road. I couldn't risk being out in the open. I ran along the side of the house until I came to the door of my secret hiding place. I shoved the board aside. It had been a long time since I had been there. The doorway seemed smaller now that I wasn't as little as I once was, but I managed to squeeze through. I sat in the center of my old spot with my knees drawn to my chest, rocking back and forth, shaking with fear just as I had as a young child.

The moonlight spilled through the cracks in the boards and shone brightly under the old house. I began to pray harder than I have ever prayed before. I asked God for guidance, to send help, anything he had to do to get this thing away from me. I heard a noise and could see a shadow moving along the side of the house. I stopped rocking and sat petrified, watching and waiting to see where it was heading.

"Angel, are you all right?" I heard a male voice whisper loudly.

Williams

I was too afraid to respond, fearing it was a trick.

"Angel, where are you? Come on, answer me, girl. I saw the lights flicker, and I am here to help."

"Mr. Sims?" I whispered. I quickly crawled over and peeked through the cracks in the boards. Sure enough, Mr. Sims stood looking up toward my bedroom window.

I opened my mouth to yell at him when another movement at the back of the house caught my eye. It was moving toward the corner, heading right for Mr. Sims. I tried to scream, but nothing came out.

Mr. Sims turned around in time to throw a punch that landed square on Mama's jaw. Only it was no longer my mother. She was fully possessed, and now this demonic thing was on the rampage searching for me. I screamed, "Run!"

Mr. Sims turned to look in my direction. At that point, Mama hit him with such force that he flew through the air, bounced off the side of the house and hit the ground like a sack of potatoes.

"Nooo!" I screamed. Tears filled my eyes, blurring my vision. He lay there motionless. It was too dark to see if he was breathing. "Get up, Mr. Sims. Please, get up," I whispered. Still, he lay there. "I am so sorry, Mr. Sims. I didn't mean for this to happen to you." I sobbed.

A loud bang startled me. Mama was trying to break into my secret hiding place underneath the house. I heard snarling and growling, but soon realized that one of Mr. Sims hunting dogs had followed him and was attacking Mama. It was dark, but I could see enough in the moonlight to tell that it was definitely a dog, and it appeared to be getting the better of her.

Mama gave up and ran off. Seeing my chance, I looked for another way out.

I saw a bright light at the lower end of the house and began crawling toward it. I remembered the flashlight, pulled it from my pocket and turned it on.

Another loud crash sounded behind me. I looked back to see this demonic creature—my mother—had busted her way into my secret spot. She was on all fours and moving fast up behind me.

I screamed and tried to crawl away, but it was too late. She grabbed me by the ankle, flipped me over on my back, and straddled me. The light flew from my hand and landed in the dirt beside me. She leaned over, her face inches from my own, her teeth clinched, seething and growling. Slobber ran down her chin and onto my face.

I somehow managed to bring my feet up, placed them around her, and kicked with all my might. She flew backward and landed a few feet away from me. She came at me again, ready to tear me apart. And this time, there was nothing I could do to stop her.

"Mama," I pleaded.

Mr. Sims' hunting dog ran in, growling and snarling. ,

He positioned himself between me and Mama.

She backed off, and for a split second, she was herself again. "Angel baby, I need you to pray for me," she said, tears forming in her eyes. "I now know that God has given you a gift, and Satan is out to destroy you because of it. I love you." She began to cry.

I sat, unable to move and unsure of how to respond to her. The dog still held his stance. I leaned over and picked up the flashlight, and shined it at Mama. The dog didn't budge. I reached out to pet him; he turned and licked my face.

"Champ, is that you, boy?" I aimed the flashlight at him.

He wagged his tail and began licking me all the more.

"Champ!" I screamed. "I can't believe it's you. I've missed you so much!" I hugged his neck and didn't want to let him go, but Mama must have moved because he went back into attack mode and stared her down.

"Angel, please, baby. There . . . isn't . . . much . . . time. Pray for me." She struggled to get the words out.

"Pray with me, Mama, okay?"

She didn't answer. She just sat there, staring straight ahead.

"Mama, repeat after me. *Dear God, forgive me of my sins.*"

"Dear God," she began. "I can't!" She sobbed. "I can't! It won't let me!"

"Mama, just try. Please!"

She sat, violently shaking her head, and once again I heard a low growl coming from within her, and it exploded into a deep demonic voice. "Your God can't help her now."

She then lay on the ground, curled in a ball. "Run, Angela!" she said with her last bit of strength. She twisted and rolled back and forth, holding her stomach.

I crawled in the direction where I'd seen a flickering light earlier. I looked back to see Champ still standing guard. He was making sure I was safe before he attempted to follow. "Come on, Champ!" I yelled.

He turned and ran to me just as I crawled out.

When I stood, I saw I was in front of the house. I thought of running toward the woods, but was afraid of getting lost or Mama seeing and following me. I heard voices coming from inside the house. Someone was walking around with a flashlight. I ran up on the porch. The front door stood wide open.

"Hello," I said in a low voice.

"Angel!" Grandma shouted. "What on earth is going on here?"

"Grandma, it's Mama."

"What about your mother?" Grandma spoke fast. "What has she done now? I mean, when she didn't show up at the bus stop, I thought maybe something was going on, and then Pastor Moore showed up on his way out of town. He decided to bring me home and make sure everything was all right here before he left town for good."

"Pastor Moore is here? Where is he?" I asked.

"He's on the back porch, checking the breakers. And... I see he found them," she said as the light flickered and came back on.

I ran into the kitchen and met the pastor at the back door. "Pastor Moore!" I shouted. "I need your help. Please help me."

"Calm down, child. What is all the fuss about?"

Grandma came in. "What's going on?"

"Grandma, listen to me, we have to get out of here." I grabbed her arm.

"Angel, calm down. We're not leaving until you tell me what's going on."

"Grandma, please! There is no time. Mama has completely lost it. She is trying to hurt me, and I thought she killed Champ, but he showed up with Mr. Sims and—"

"What are you talking about? And where is Mr. Sims?" Grandma asked.

"Oh! My gosh, I forgot about Mr. Sims. Mama attacked him. He fell and isn't moving."

"Jud Sims? Oh lord." Grandma nervously picked up the phone and called 911. "Send an ambulance!" she shouted, giving our address. She hung up the phone and yelled over her shoulder to Pastor Moore, "Keep an eye on Angel while I check on Mr. Sims."

She ran out the back door.

I turned, facing the pastor. I didn't know how to explain what was going on. It all sounded crazy and unreal, even to me.

Grandma returned a few minutes later to inform us that Mr. Sims was badly injured but conscious. She then grabbed both my arms, looked me in the eyes, and sternly asked, "Where is your mother?"

Before I could answer, Champ, who was standing guard on the front porch, began to growl. I shouted for him to come to me. He ran into the house, and I grabbed him by the collar, led him to the bathroom and locked him in. I wasn't taking any chances of losing him again. I heard someone walk up the stairs and onto the front porch.

Just as I suspected, it was Mama. She walked through the door covered in blood and her clothes torn partially off.

Grandma gasped, placing her hand over her mouth.

"Dear God, Margret! What has happened to you?" Grandma started to go to her, but Pastor Moore threw his hand out, stopping her. "Don't. She is not your daughter."

Grandma had been to church and read the bible enough to know what the pastor meant by that. She began to cry.

"Get a hold of yourself," the pastor said to Grandma. "I need you to go into the kitchen and bring me a chair and something I can use to tie her up."

Grandma stood there dumbfounded.

"Hurry!"

Grandma rushed into the kitchen and returned moments later with a chair and a rope and handed them to the pastor. He grabbed Mama by the arm, shoved her down on the chair, and, with Grandma's help, proceeded to tie her up.

I never moved from my spot in front of the bathroom. Champ was clawing at the door, trying to dig his way out.

Mama sat quietly with downcast eyes. She didn't attempt to stop them. Just as the last rope was being secured, her head dropped lower. The only part of her that moved were those demonic black eyes. They rolled into the back of her head, and then rolled back down and looked at the pastor. An evil grin spread across her face. She spoke in a voice that was not her own. It was the same one I had heard earlier. Deep and menacing. "Do you think that can hold me, pastor? You pathetic piece of—"

"Shut up!" the pastor yelled.

"Why don't you join us?" it said. This thing was no longer my mother.

Pastor Moore ignored the question and began reciting the Lord's Prayer.

Grandma ran to her room and came back with a Bible. She handed it to the pastor.

He opened it and began to read, only to be interrupted each time.

"Hey, Pastor! Your wife and daughter are in here with us, remember them? Or have you forgotten already?" It smirked.

"I said shut up!" the pastor shouted once again.

"Remember hearing the screams of your wife Laura and your daughter Emily? Ah, poor sweet little Emily, lying there at the side of the road fighting for breath, in a pool of blood, waiting for Daddy to come to the rescue and pray to his God for help."

"I said shut your foul mouth," shouted Pastor Moore as he rushed over and grabbed Mama by the throat.

The demon laughed.

"Go ahead, pastor. Kill her. You know you want to. You didn't save your wife and daughter, so here is your chance to save another little girl."

The pastor released his grip and backed off without looking away.

"Do it, you good for nothing coward," it shouted.

Pastor Moore regained his composure and started praying again.

All the while, the demon cursed and tried to disrupt his prayers.

"Hey, pastor, want some of this?" It ran its hand up Mama's leg and under her dress. "Come on, take it. Do what you want to her. She won't remember a thing; we have total control of her now." It stuck out its tongue and licked it's bloody, disgusting lips.

Sirens wailed from somewhere down the road.

"Well, well, is that sirens I hear coming, pastor? Let's see how this plays out. Here I am, a poor defenseless woman strapped to a chair, bloody and injured. Needing help. And you tried to choke me to death. Yeah, this is going to look terrible on your part. But I think you will like jail, pastor, and you might enjoy playing drop the soap in the shower." It reared its head back and laughed sadistically.

The ambulance pulled into the driveway, followed by a police car. Two officers stepped out and shined a flashlight around the perimeter.

Pastor Moore told Grandma to meet them outside and take them to Mr. Sims, which she did without hesitation.

While Pastor Moore kept Mama's attention, I slid back against the wall and carefully made my way toward the front door, then onto the porch with Grandma.

"Hello, ma'am," said a female officer as she met Grandma in front of the house. "I'm Officer Burns. Are you the one who called?"

"Yes, I did," Grandma answered. "My daughter is inside. She … she's… it's hard to explain, but—"

We heard a loud moan around the side of the house.

"What was that?" the officer asked.

"It's Jud Sims, our neighbor, and he's badly injured. He's over there." She led the way.

Mr. Sims was sitting against the house when the paramedics got to him. He tried to get up but screamed out in pain.

"Sir," the first paramedic, a heavy-set man with curly red hair and beard, said. "I need you to sit still and tell me where the pain is."

"My leg and right shoulder." Mr. Sims gritted his teeth as he spoke.

"How bad are his injuries?" asked Officer Burns. "We need to ask him a few questions."

"Not sure. Possible broken leg and collarbone. We need to get him to the hospital to be examined," the paramedic answered.

The paramedics loaded Mr. Sims on a gurney and began strapping him on it.

Officer Burns took down Mr. Sims' information, which wasn't much because it was dark, and he couldn't see what or who had attacked him.

Meanwhile, Officer Wells talked with Grandma to collaborate the stories. Officer Burns returned with questions of her own.

Officer Wells took his partner aside and whispered, "Isn't she the crazy lady who keeps coming to the station claiming her daughter is psycho?"

"Now that you mention it, I do believe you're right," Officer Burns replied. "I knew this was going to be a strange night, and I have a feeling it's only going to get weirder."

The clouds moved, and the moon shone brightly.

"There is the problem," Officer Burns said, pointing up at the sky. "A full moon always brings out the crazies."

"Yeah, well, I guess it beats sitting on the roadside waiting to catch someone for speeding." Officer Wells laughed. "Let's get this over with so I can get home. My wife called to say dinner was waiting, and I'm starving."

Grandma and I stood at the foot of the stairs waiting for the officers to catch up. She was just about to explain to the best of her ability what was happening inside the house when Mama shouted for help.

"Keep an eye on them while I check this out." Officer Wells pulled out his gun and ran onto the porch, followed by Officer Burns, Grandma, and me. He stopped at the door with his back pressed against the wall. "Police! Is everything all right in there?"

Grandma whispered, "It's not what it seems. I have been trying to tell you that my daughter needs help, and now maybe you will believe me."

Both officers nervously peeked around the door, being careful before stepping inside.

The demonic thing turned and spoke in my mother's voice, "Please help. They are trying to kill me." She pretended to cry.

"Okay, ma'am, everything is going to be all right. We're here to help," Officer Wells said.

"What is going on here?" Officer Burns asked upon seeing Mama strapped to a chair. "Where is the little girl?"

"I'm right here," I said, stepping forward.

Mama swung her head around and stared at me with a look of pure hate and evil all in one.

I ran to the bathroom door to calm Champ, who was still scratching and growling. I didn't dare open the door for fear he may attack Mama and get shot by one of the officers.

"Jim Wells, is that you?" Pastor Moore asked.

"Pastor Moore? I thought you left town a long time ago. What's going on here? We got a call that someone was attacked and found one victim lying outside, and now you have a woman who is clearly in need of medical attention tied to a chair. Would you care to explain yourself?"

"Jim, I have known your family since you were a baby, and you know I would never harm a fly. But I need you to leave this situation to God and me; this isn't something you can deal with."

"Sorry, but I can't do that, pastor. This woman is in fear for her life and badly in need of medical attention. Chris, go get the paramedics in here now."

Officer Burns stepped out the door just as the paramedics finished loading Mr. Sims into the ambulance.

"We have another one in here," she shouted.

Both paramedics rushed in to find Mama bloody and begging for help. They started toward her.

Pastor Moore held up his hand. "Stop! Don't go near her."

They stopped and looked at each other. "Sir, we have to make sure she's all right. She needs to get those cuts checked out, and from here it appears that she will need stitches."

"This woman is demonically possessed. I know that you may not believe that or even understand it, but I am telling you the truth." Pastor Moore reached into his shirt pocket and pulled out a small bottle of anointing oil.

"Hold it right there!" Officer Burns shouted. "What's in your hand?"

The officer looked at her partner, and he motioned for her to position herself on the other side of Mama.

He then turned to Pastor Moore, his gun still drawn and pointing at him. "Please, pastor, don't make me shoot you. Just let the lady go, and you can give a full statement at the police station."

Mama began crying and spewing out the most god-awful lies. She was so believable that I almost fell for her pathetic act.

"I asked you a question." Officer Burns said. "What's in the vial?"

"It's anointing oil." Pastor Moore held it up to show everyone, then placed his finger on the top and tipped it. Oil ran out on his finger and down the side toward the palm of his hand. He took a few steps, stopped in front of Mama, and held up his finger to show everyone.

Mama became agitated, shouting and cursing at him to get away from her.

He ignored her as he placed a cross on her forehead, saying, "In the name of the Father, the Son and the Holy Ghost."

Mama let out a high-pitched scream.

Both officers now had their guns drawn. One of the paramedics rushed to her to try and help.

She turned her head in his direction and growled a deep, demonic growl unlike the ones before. This one was much eviler. She busted the chair apart and leapt up on all fours on the back of the couch, twisting her head in ways that are humanly impossible.

"Oh, hell, no! I didn't sign up for this!" Officer Burns shouted and ran out the door, locking herself in the car.

Both paramedics followed Burns out the door and left toward the hospital with Mr. Sims.

"Jim, if you're staying here, I need your help to strap her down," Pastor Moore shouted above all the growling and demonic noises.

The officer stood frozen, unable to move or speak.

"Help me hold her down, Jim!" Pastor Moore shouted.

The officer grabbed her and threw her down on the couch and held her there.

She looked up at him and smiled. "I always thought you were hot, officer." Her slimy tongue shot out and licked up the left side of his face.

Officer Wells cringed and rubbed his face on his shoulder. He knew better than to turn her loose.

Pastor Moore returned from the kitchen with a metal chair that Mama kept in the corner. They wrestled her onto it and worked to open zip ties to secure her with.

Mama continued spewing curse words and lies at them.

I took a step forward.

Her head shot sideways and she glared at me with hatred in her eyes.

Somehow, she broke free again. Within seconds, she grabbed the officer's gun. She turned and pressed it between my eyes.

A voice spoke in my ear. "Fear not, for I am always with you. You have the power within you." I felt a breeze blow through me, and all fear subsided. I reached up and pulled the gun from her hand.

The officer and the pastor grabbed her, and this time made sure she was strapped down before letting go of her. She grinned, leaned her head back, and levitated about five feet off the floor. The chair slowly came back down. She looked up with a grin and began speaking in Latin.

For some reason, I understood every word.

"What did she say?" the officer asked.

"It's Latin, and I have no idea what she said," Pastor Moore answered.

I stepped in front of her, never taking my eyes off her. "She said, 'I have been here long before this world stood, and I will be here long after it's gone. You are all going to die tonight.'"

She spat on me and began laughing and cursing. "Angel! Stay back!" shouted Pastor Moore.

I handed the gun to Officer Wells. He aimed it at her, ready to shoot should she make another move toward me.

Her head turned in his direction, an evil grin spread across her face. "Go ahead and shoot, you fucking coward." Slobber ran down her chin and clung in slimy strings on her shirt. She reared back her head and laughed.

I held up my hand to signal Officer Wells to wait.

"Step back, kid. Very slowly," the officer said, his gun still drawn.

Pastor Moore continued reading from the bible. I have no idea how Champ got out of the bathroom, but he stepped in front of me, teeth barred, growling, his hair standing on end. I reached for his collar, intending on pulling him back as I shouted, "Jesus help us!"

No sooner had the words crossed my lips, a flash of bright light flashed, and the room began to swirl. Wind blew through the living room, papers blew and twirled around the room like a tornado, the curtains stood straight out and waved like a flag on a flagpole. Then things grew deathly quiet.

Pastor Moore's mouth still moved as he read from the bible, the wind still blew, papers continued twirling. Champ held his ground, teeth barred, ears pinned back, neck and back bristled. Officer Wells shouted something I couldn't hear. It was as though everything was moving in slow motion. I didn't realize I was moving until I stood in front of Mama, staring this thing in the eyes.

I felt a strength come over me and heard words ringing in my ears. "It's time." I placed my hand on her forehead and spoke the words that I heard playing over and over in my head. I spoke them with boldness and faith in God because I knew He was going to take care of everything, right here and now. "You foul demon, I know your name, and why you're here. You are no longer in control of this woman or this family."

"Nooo! Leave us alone!" it screamed.

"In the name of Jesus Christ, the Son of God, I command you to come out!" I shouted.

Mama's head shot back, her mouth opened, and, with a loud scream, her body went limp and her head dropped forward. A few minutes went by before she raised her head and smiled the most beautiful smile I had ever seen.

Her eyes were as dark blue as my own and Grandma's.

Our prayers had been answered. I would no longer have to fear Mama; no longer have to fear her moods. The darkness that had hovered over our home was gone, and I knew in my soul it was gone for good.

EPILOGUE

Mama and I took counseling for a while to heal our relationship. I forgave her for everything; she asked God to forgive her, and she has finally forgiven herself. I learned that Mama blamed me for Daddy's death. We were on our way home after having dinner in town. The ride home was quiet; the only noise was the hum of the motor and the tires hitting the pavement. I slept peacefully in my car seat until I was stung by a bee. I woke up screaming. It startled Daddy, causing him to lose control of the car and slam head-on into a tree, killing him instantly. Mama became so lonely and depressed that she began playing around with witchcraft in hopes of making contact with him.

We no longer live in the house on the mountain. Mama wanted to make a fresh start, and thus had the house torn down and sold the property.

I am now grown and will be twenty-four in a few months. I am a loyal member of Pastor Moore's little country church and work with him on cases like mine.

That's my story, and here I sit in that little country church. The service is coming to a close. Grandma's hand still lay on mine, and she taps to the beat of the music as the choir prepares to sing the closing song.

I look to the right and smile at Mama. I love the sparkle in her eyes. I am so proud of the person she is today. We have been through so much, but by the grace of God, we were able to forgive and move past all the bad times. I learned that it's best to let the past stay in the past. It doesn't do any good to dwell on it. It can't be reversed, but through God's love and forgiveness, we can choose how we live our lives. I chose to use the gift God placed on me to help others.

I reach over and take Mama by the hand. "That's your cue," I said.

She smiles, hugs me, and walks to the front of the church, taking her place with the choir. Pastor Moore hands her a microphone, and she sings in the most angelic voice anyone has ever heard. She has been an active member of the church since the day she was delivered from the demon. She also travels from state to state, speaking on the dangers of messing with witchcraft and the occult.

The song ends. Pastor Moore approaches me, smiles and asks if I am ready to go.

Williams

"I sure am. You know I keep a bag packed and ready to go in the trunk of my car, so where to this time?" I ask as we step outside the church.

"Iowa," Pastor Moore says, and then adds, "Possible demonic possession of a twelve-year-old boy. The doctors say it's a mental condition and wants to institutionalize him, but his parents believe otherwise. That's where you come in. You seem to be the only one who can see as well as hear these things."

"Now, now, pastor. You also have the gift—if you just learn to open your heart and mind to it."

"We just need you to evaluate the boy and let them know if it is something medical or—"

"Or what?" I ask.

"Nothing, our job is to evaluate him and that's it."

"Pastor Moore, what are you saying? You know the same God who gives us the power to cast out demons is the same God who can also heal any medical condition.— If this boy needs help, I refuse to walk away. My conscience wouldn't allow it, and if I know you as well as I think I do, neither will yours." "Yes, Angel, you are right," Pastor Moore replies.

Grandma grabs my hand squeezes it. "Go get 'em, girl." She hugs me tightly.

Mama comes out, kisses my forehead, and then she and Grandma say a prayer with us.

I take my seat on the front passenger side. Pastor Moore starts the car and drives away.

I roll down my window and shout, "Take care of Champ for me. He isn't as young as he used to be, you know." I throw my hand out the window and wave to them until we're out of sight.

Iowa, here we come.

Made in the USA
Middletown, DE
14 May 2022